SHOWDOWN

Surprise was now his only ally, and with six shells in the pistol and five targets, it was almost a standoff. Slocum knew that one man could handle several—as long as none of them is willing to die . . .

One of them saw him immediately. His startled reaction caused the others to turn.

Softly, Slocum whispered, "Gents, lose your guns."

OTHER BOOKS BY JAKE LOGAN

JAKE LOGAN

COLORADO KILLERS

BERKLEY BOOKS, NEW YORK

COLORADO KILLERS

A Berkley Book/published by arrangement with
the author

PRINTING HISTORY
Berkley edition/February 1990

ISBN: 0-425-11971-8

A BERKLEY BOOK ® TM 757,375
Berkley Books are published by The Berkley Publishing Group,
200 Madison Avenue, New York, New York 10016.
The name "BERKLEY" and the "B" logo
are trademarks belonging to Berkley Publishing Corporation.

PRINTED IN THE UNITED STATES OF AMERICA

10 9 8 7 6 5 4 3 2 1

1

The high sky looked as if it stretched to the end of the earth. John Slocum draped his arms over his saddle horn and watched a solitary cloud glide through the trackless blue that stretched from as far behind as he could see to the very tips of the mountains to the far west. The sun was a brighter yellow than he'd seen in a long time, so bright it was almost white.

Slocum turned in his saddle, the squeak of leather the only noise on the ridge, and looked down the winding trail he had followed up the low mountain. A sea of grass, bending before the wind, changed color from a dull green to a shiny silver and back again as a single breath of air moved across the valley as if an invisible hand stroked the fur of a sleeping cat.

He thought of Georgia, where he'd been born, and the mountains of Tennessee, but there was nothing like this glorious vista in either state. The West was something special. The endless plains, oceans of sweet water, and mountains only God could climb never ceased to amaze him. He felt almost pure out here, but not quite. Too much had happened, too much that he couldn't forget, and much that he still didn't understand. There were times when he thought his life was a puzzle designed for someone to enjoy.

But the West was as good an anesthetic as he could find. It didn't kill the pain, not completely, but it gave him some peace, reduced it to a dull throb, like a toothache on the way out. It wasn't perfect, but he'd stopped looking for perfection a long time ago. What he needed was a place where he could redefine himself, strip away the past that clung to him like red dirt on a Georgia farmer's skin. The West was the place, it was the opportunity. The rest was up to him. He knew there were no guarantees, but he didn't want any, would have been offended by the idea. All he wanted was a chance.

Slocum kicked his mount in the flanks, using the sides of his heels rather than the spurs. There had been enough of that, enough coercion, enough pressure. No reason to lean on an animal that had done everything he'd asked of it. Patting the big stallion's neck, he tangled his fingers in the thick reddish mane and leaned back as the horse began to descend to the valley in front of him.

The valley was shaped like a broad, shallow vee, full of grass from ridge to ridge, except at the very bottom, where a wide, shallow river meandered uncertainly through it from end to end. To the south, it broadened into a small lake. The water was darker than the sky, stealing color from the heavens and adding it to its own bright blue. Stands of cottonwood and juniper marked nearly every bend and rimmed the lake. The sun glittered on the surface, sparkling where the river broke over rocks in its course, and where the gentle wind rippled the lake.

For a moment, Slocum thought about what a perfect place it would be to farm. But the thought didn't last long. He couldn't settle down, not yet, not until he figured out who he was. And he knew he couldn't do that standing still. He had to move, to find that place where the knowledge of who he really was, and what he was supposed to do, was waiting for him.

As the roan stepped carefully through the knee-high grass, he filed the first vista of the valley away with a hundred others. It was a possibility for later. Someday: that seemed to be the story of his life. Someday maybe he could come back here and sink a plow in the earth. Someday he could cut timber and build himself someplace to stay, someplace solid, someplace permanent. But not yet.

It was the middle of the day, about a half hour after noon. Slocum was hungry and he was thirsty. He pushed the horse a little harder, anxious to make camp and climb down out of the saddle for an hour or two. He looked up again at the cloud, a little farther east on its leisurely tour. It had changed shape now, stretched out thin and tattered at the edges, as if something were tearing at it. Even up there, Slocum thought, things you can't see won't leave you alone.

He was on the bottom now, and the slope was almost nonexistent. The grass was taller. The tough stems of paintbrush and columbine made the going heavier. The horse shied away from an especially thick patch of thorny thistle, shaking off the reins and skipping to the left a few paces before plunging on toward the nearest stand of cottonwoods. The closer he got, the louder the river sounded, and Slocum realized just how long it had been since he had a mouthful of cold water.

Close to the cottonwoods, tangled underbrush made the going even tougher. Slocum spurred the big stallion through the brush and broke through to the riverbank. A strip of rocky soil, fifteen or twenty feet wide, its grass little more than puffs here and there, grated under the horse's hooves, and Slocum dismounted. He tethered the animal to a cottonwood limb, then moved downstream to gather an armload of small branches, enough to build a small fire and keep it going for an hour or so. It was warm, but he wanted coffee and some hot food.

He used a handful of dry grass for tinder, then fed a few twigs to the smoldering blaze. As the smoke turned to a bright blue flame, he boxed some medium branches around it, breaking several over his knee, then waited until the heavier wood caught fire. Once the fire was in no danger of going out, he walked back to the horse and jerked his Winchester out of its boot.

Moving back through the trees, Slocum headed up into the grass. He'd seen a few grouse and quail on the way down, and a couple of rabbits. A slice of venison would have been better, but Slocum wasn't about to kill a deer for a single steak. A big rabbit, startled by his footsteps, froze for a second, then zigzagged off through the weeds before he could get the Winchester up.

This was Cheyenne country, and he didn't want to fire any more than necessary. One shot would be best, but he didn't kid himself that that was going to be possible. He flushed another rabbit, again too late for a clear shot, but the rabbit chased a brace of quail. Slocum aimed carefully, going for the first bird. They angled off to the left, and he led his shot a little and squeezed. The crack seemed to slap back at him, bouncing off the sky and losing much of its energy as the bird broke the smooth flap of its wings and tumbled down like an old rag.

The second quail veered off to the right, then dove back into the grass. Slocum sprinted toward the downed bird, using the stock of the rifle to sweep away the grass. It took several minutes before he found a smear of fresh blood, then he had to track the bird another ten yards before he found it, lying on its back, its eyes still open, glittering in the sunlight, the clear membranes pulsing feebly. Slocum bent to grab it and realized he'd just barely nailed it with a wing shot. The broken bone protruded through a tuft of bloody feathers up near the shoulder.

Halfheartedly, the dying bird scratched at the back of his hand with feeble claws. The uninjured wing fluttered against his wrist as he hauled it out of the tall grass. Slocum twisted the quail's neck sharply, and the good wing stopped flapping. Holding the bird at arm's length, he turned back to the river. A thin column of blue-gray smoke wound up through the cottonwoods as Slocum headed for the fire.

Too hungry for subtlety, Slocum seared the feathers off the dead bird. He cut off the head, gutted it and washed it clean in the river. Spitting the bird on a green branch, he dropped the quail onto a pair of forked sticks, then sat back and watched the fire.

The horse whinnied as the smell of the cooking bird drifted toward it. Slocum was bone-tired. He lay back, his arms folded behind his head, and watched the cottonwoods bend in the slight breeze. It was tempting to forget that he was out of work, even more tempting to ignore the twenty dollars in his pocket, the last twenty dollars he could call his own. Colorado was supposed to be a place where a man could turn things around. He hoped it was true, but didn't want to bank on it. If he had a dollar for every place that was supposed to be the nearest thing to Eden, he wouldn't need a job at all.

The cooking quail smelled good. Grease from the bird started to drip into the flames, making them sputter and the smoke to thicken and turn dark. He sat up to check on the bird, then got on his knees and crawled over to the fire to turn the spit a little. The skin on the underside was charred black and starting to blister off. He picked at the skin and popped a strip in his mouth. The charcoal taste was bitter, but he was too hungry to worry about it, and peeled another strip, exposing the dark meat of a leg, already nearly done.

He lay back again, tucking his arms under his head and tilting his hat forward. He heard the first shot without realizing what it was. There was no mistaking the second, followed closely by a third. Slocum jumped and listened. At first he thought it might have been a hunter, or a cowboy like himself, bringing down an afternoon meal. But the next rapid flurry of rifle shots told him just how wrong he had been.

The gunfire was at the northern end of the valley. He couldn't see anything through the cottonwoods on the far side of the river. Forgetting all about the quail, he got to his feet and raced to his horse. Kicking the stallion back through the underbrush, he heard the first distant cries, piercing and barely human. The sound drifted toward him on the wind in bits and pieces. He still wasn't sure what he was hearing as he charged up the slope to get above the tree line.

The cries were more insistent now, and Slocum turned in the saddle to see where they were coming from. Halfway up the slope, he reined in to stand in the stirrups. More gunshots cracked at the mouth of the valley. On the far side of the river, where it broke through a notch in the rolling foothills, Slocum spotted the familiar canvas cover of a wagon. The wagon was moving fast, rolling over the dry earth on the riverbank. He wheeled his horse just as a band of Cheyenne broke over the hilltop and charged down toward the river.

Now he knew where the cries were coming from as the

Cheyenne whooped and hollered, their horses going at a full gallop over the gentle slope. They were firing again, but the guns were aimed in the air. They seemed more intent on terrifying the occupants of the wagon than anything else. Five hundred yards behind the wagon, they were slowly closing the gap. When they got close enough, Slocum knew, they would turn their rifles on the wagon.

Slocum kicked his horse into a trot, heading back down toward the riverbank. Once he hit the flat bottom land, he could open it up. Breaking through the underbrush, he urged the stallion across the bank and out into the shallow river. He had no idea how deep the water might be at the middle of the river, but this was no time for caution. The cold water climbed up his legs, numbing his feet and calves. The horse launched itself into chest-deep water, and, when it could not longer touch bottom, it started to swim. Slocum was content to hang on and let the animal's natural instincts carry it to safety on the far bank.

When its hooves touched bottom again, the big roan floundered for a moment until it found secure footing. The horse hauled itself into shallow water and Slocum used the spurs again to kick it up onto the bank.

The river's course was too erratic for Slocum to see anything upstream. He pushed the roan, hoping the wagon kept to the water's edge. The gunshots were less sporadic now, more deliberate, as if the Cheyenne had settled into some serious marksmanship. Slocum hauled the Winchester out of its boot as he rounded a bend in the river. Far ahead, at the opposite end of a big, looping curve in the river, he caught a glimpse of the wagon for a second as it plunged through a gap in the trees.

The wagon was rocking from side to side, its big wheels sinking into the soft earth and slowing it down. A moment later, the Cheyenne, six of them, burst into the clearing. They were only a hundred yards behind the wagon now.

Even as he kicked the roan harder, he wondered whether he was too late.

2

Slocum skidded to a halt a hundred yards in front of the wagon. Jerking his saddlebags off the rear of his saddle, he glanced upriver. Then he let the horse go, chasing it into the trees with a yip and a wave of his hat. The frightened animal shied away and plunged into a thick clump of cottonwoods. Slocum urged the wagon on with a windmilling of his dusty Stetson.

The cloud of dust billowing up behind the wagon obscured the Cheyenne, but he could still hear the thunder of their horses' hooves. The wagon creaked and groaned as its exhausted team fought fatigue and the soft dirt. The wheels dragged more than they turned, and the driver, a woman in workshirt and straw hat, snapped the reins relentlessly, urging her team on.

Slocum waited until the wagon was almost on top of him before hurling himself to one side and taking cover behind a fallen tree. The wagon roared past, the iron rims of its creaking wheels scattering sparks from the loose rock. A shower of pebbles pelted Slocum's back and shoulders, then a cloud of fine dust sifted down over him. The Cheyenne were saving their ammunition now. Through the thinning plume of dust, he could see them like silhouettes in a shadow play.

Jerking a round into the chamber, he sighted in with the Winchester, holding the rifle steady and waiting for the right moment. Rather than kill one of the Indians, he wanted to send them a message. If they could understand it, fine, nobody got hurt. If not, well . . . he'd cross that bridge when and if he had to.

Holding his breath, he squeezed off a shot, catching the

lead pony low on the chest, just above the knee joint. The animal stumbled. Wreathed in a beige cloud, the tumble looked like a minstrel show pratfall, ass over elbows. The remaining horses split into two groups and swept past the fallen brave and his crippled mount. Slocum shrugged, debating whether to go for a second horse or up the ante. The braves were too close for much hesitation, and Slocum raised his sights and squeezed off a second shot, quickly jerking another shell home. His target fell backward off his horse, and the trailing brave narrowly missed stepping on him as he roared by.

Rolling to his left, Slocum crawled around the huge clump of dirt and tangled roots at the base of the tree and swung the Winchester around as the Cheyenne galloped by. One of the braves wheeled his horse in a tight circle and charged back in his direction. Still scrambling for cover, Slocum fired a wild shot that took the horse down. The Cheyenne tumbled forward as the pony's front legs collapsed and Slocum ran toward the Indian, his rifle raised high overhead. As the Indian tried to recover, Slocum slammed the Winchester butt-first between his shoulder blades. The impact made a sickening thud and the shock tore at Slocum's shoulder joints. The brave collapsed with a groan.

The wagon had stopped about a hundred and fifty yards downriver. Someone in the rear was returning fire now, and the Cheyenne reined in. The Indians dismounted and scattered into the trees. Scattered fire broke out along the line of cottonwoods, and Slocum could see the slugs chipping at the wagon bed. Twice the canvas cover dimpled, then popped back as a bullet passed on through and out the far side of the canvas.

So far, they had two wounded and two horses down. If anything, all that had done was make the Cheyenne more determined than ever to get at the wagon and its occupants. Slocum didn't know quite where he would fit into their plans, but he'd be damned if he'd wait around to find out. Dodging in among the trees, he found his own horse cowering in the underbrush. He tethered the roan, scooped a

box of shells for the rifle out of the saddlebags, and draped
them back over the horse.

Zigzagging through the stand of trees, Slocum cut in
behind the Cheyenne, getting just close enough to see the
last brave, flat on the ground and squirming through the
underbrush. Slocum dropped to one knee and drew a bead
on the Cheyenne's head, then led him just a little too
much. He still didn't want to kill anyone if he didn't have
to. Slocum raised his sights a little and clipped a small
branch over the brave's head. The startled Indian jerked his
head around, and Slocum held a hand up, palm toward the
Cheyenne. The Indian knew Slocum could have killed him
and he seemed to resent it. But he climbed to his feet,
leaving his rifle on the ground.

Slowly the brave walked toward Slocum, his hands at
his sides as if to say this was a meeting of equals rather
than potential victim and big-hearted could-be assassin.
Slocum was trying to decide whether he could talk to the
brave and, if so, what he could say, but the Indian saved
him the trouble. Jerking his right hand so fast Slocum only
saw a blur, the Indian flipped a knife that narrowly missed
Slocum as it flew by. Watching the knife, he lost the Indian. The brave had vanished into the sparse trees.

Slocum eased toward the river, unwilling to let the Indian circle in behind him. As he stepped out of the brush,
he realized the firing had stopped. Downstream, the three
remaining Indians were back on their horses. With the pre-
cision of a drill team, they wheeled their horses in unison
and thundered back in Slocum's direction. Fifty yards
downriver, the last brave darted out of the trees, his recovered rifle draped over his shoulder on a buckskin sling, and
climbed up behind the middle brave.

The lead Cheyenne brought his rifle around and fired at
Slocum, more to make a point than to hit him, and Slocum
dropped and rolled, losing his hat and tangling himself in
the brush. Before he could recover, the Cheyenne were
past him, and he decided not to renew hostilities.

The remaining two Cheyenne, one bleeding profusely
from a shoulder wound, galloped into the open, taking the
lead for a few moments, until the two single-rider ponies

rushed past. The two-man ponies brought up the rear now and in a minute, just the distant clap of their hooves remained. Then it, too, was gone. Slocum heaved a sigh, bent to retrieve his hat, and clapped his pants with it to chase the dust.

He ducked into the trees to retrieve his own horse, then secured the saddlebags and remounted. He braced the Winchester across his saddle and nudged the still skittish animal out into the open. The horse seemed reluctant to move, and Slocum had to jerk the reins sharply to remind the big roan which one of them wore the bit.

The wagon had started moving again and was already another fifty yards downriver. Slocum wondered for a moment who could have been that ungrateful. He thought for a second about shrugging it off, then, cursing to himself, urged the roan forward. He'd be damned if he'd let such a breach of etiquette go unremarked. The least the bastards could do was wave a hat or something to show their appreciation.

Settling into a fast trot, the roan closed the gap fairly quickly. With fifty yards to go, Slocum shouted to get the wagon's attention, but no one responded. He closed another ten yards and shouted a second. He still got no response. Once more, he was tempted to write it off, chalking the whole affair up to rudeness and letting it go at that.

But he was angry now and thought a thank you, even one clearly not meant, was the least he deserved for sticking his neck out. It wasn't lost on him, either, that he still had a couple of hundred miles to go through Cheyenne country. Word traveled fast, and even though the Indians were no longer the threat they once were, the foothills of the Rockies were still dotted with small villages who either hadn't gotten the word or didn't give a damn. Not that there was any reason the Cheyenne should care, but the Indian wars were all but over and it was about time to bury the remaining hatchets someplace other than a white man's skull.

Slocum had put himself in some little jeopardy, whether

the wagoneers knew it or not. His sense of propriety was offended, and he wanted satisfaction. Kicking the roan, he drove toward the rear of the wagon when a single shot cracked. The slug narrowly missed him, whining past his ear and slamming into a tree to his right rear.

Slocum reined in and shouted again. "Hey, what the hell's wrong with you people?"

"Go away," a woman's voice shouted back. "We know why you're here."

"The hell you do," Slocum shouted.

"You tell McDonald to leave us alone. That sonofabitch better quit while he still can."

"Hold on, now," Slocum shouted. "I don't know any McDonald. I don't know what you're talking about."

Another rifle shot cracked from the rear of the wagon. This one came nowhere near him, but he was too angry to care. There was rudeness and then there was downright rudeness. But he'd never seen anything like this.

"Lady, I don't know what the hell you're trying to do, but I just put myself out on a limb for you. The least you could do is say thanks."

"Thanks," she shouted, then cut loose with a third shot. This one was too close, skipping off a stone just to the roan's left and sending slivers of quartz off into the trees.

Slocum kicked the horse flat out and covered the remaining distance in a few seconds. If the woman doing the shooting had changed her mind, he'd be okay. If not, he doubted she could hit him by anything other than a freak accident. Still, accidents do happen, and he kept well to the left, just above the waterline until he was right alongside the wagon.

He urged the roan in toward the wagon, now, and slowed to a walk when he came abreast of the front seat. the woman at the reins glanced at him, then clucked to her exhausted team. A rifle barrel poked out of the rear, just over the woman's shoulder. Slocum saw it and ducked. But the gunman didn't fire again.

"You better give those animals some rest," Slocum said. "You're about to kill them."

"Why, so the rest of your friends can catch up to us?"

"What are talking about? The rest of what friends?" Slocum was bewildered, and the woman at the reins seemed finally to believe him. She tugged on the reins, and the tired horses gratefully slowed to a walk, then stopped altogether.

"You really don't know Kevin McDonald?"

Slocum shook his head. "Cross my heart," he said, grinning to try to put her at ease.

The woman kicked on the brake and looped the reins around the brake handle. "Then I guess we do owe you an apology."

"I think that's an understatement," Slocum said. "Now, who's this McDonald?"

"You really don't know?"

"Never heard of him."

The woman grabbed the brim of her hat and pulled it off, shaking loose a head of the reddest hair Slocum had ever seen. It tumbled down over her shoulders and reached nearly to the wagon seat. She fixed him with a crystal-clear, steady blue gaze for a long moment. "If you're lying to me, I swear to God, I'll kill you, if I have to use my bare hands. I swear."

Slocum held up both hands to show he was the soul of honesty. The woman nodded. She jumped gracefully out of the wagon, landing lightly and striding immediately toward the rear of the wagon. She undid the retaining pins on the tailgate, rattling the chains against the bullet-splintered wood.

The canvas cover parted as she lowered the tailgate. A rifle barrel poked out of the shadows for a second, then a second woman, like the first dressed in jeans and a denim shirt, dropped to the ground. She, too, had long red hair. The second passenger followed her out, and Slocum found himself staring at yet a third young woman. Her hair was just as long, but blue-black in color. Slocum wondered whether he was drunk. He looked at the driver, but her face was expressionless.

He started to say something when she barked, "Karen, come on out here."

Now he knew he was drunk and wondered where he could get some more of whatever it was that had gotten him there. When Karen, her blond hair in a thick braid all he way to her waist, hit the ground, Slocum decided water would do.

3

Slocum looked at the four women. They were young and they were attractive. Why were they on their own in a wagon, in Cheyenne country? The driver seemed to sense his thoughts.

"Don't go getting any ideas, cowboy," she said, taking a rifle from the blonde. "We wouldn't be here if men like you didn't get ideas like you're getting right now."

Slocum shook his head. "No ideas, I promise."

"But . . . ?"

"But I was just wondering why you were out here in the middle of nowhere. All by yourselves."

"We were doing alright."

"Past tense is appropriate. You were just about to stop doing alright."

"Don't be so full of yourself. We're not little girls."

"I can see that . . ."

"Well, forget it. We're grateful, but not *that* grateful."

"I don't mean that. I just meant that those Cheyenne were about to change your luck."

The woman with black hair stepped toward him, one hand extended. "Don't be so hard on him, Liz. He *did*, after all, help. I hate to think what might have happened if he hadn't come along." Slocum took her hand. The grip was firm and her skin was taut and cool. "Barbara McDonough," she said. "Thank you, Mr. . . . ?"

"Slocum," he said, shaking her hand, "John Slocum."

"Thank you, Mr. Slocum, for all of us." She looked pointedly at the woman she called Liz. "The angry hornet is Liz Holcom." Turning to the blonde who stepped forward and extended her own hand, she said, "This is Karen

15

Yeager." Karen shook his hand less vigorously, averting her eyes the whole time, then stepped back to lean against the wagon. "And this is Mabel Shaw," McDonough said, indicating the second redhead. Mabel nodded but said nothing and did not offer to shake Slocum's hand.

"We really are grateful, Mr. Slocum. Honestly. I guess we're all a little frightened, that's all."

"Pleased to meet you, ladies. Glad to help. I guess I was a little put out when you ran off. But I suppose it's none of my business why."

Slocum walked back to his horse. He climbed into the saddle and turned to wave good-bye. Barbara looked as if she was on the verge of saying something, but a glance from Liz Holcom silenced her. Slocum nodded and urged his mount toward the river. Downstream, he could see the plume of smoke from his fire and remembered the quail, now probably burnt beyond recognition, let alone edibility.

The roan was knee-deep in the river when Liz called out, "Mr. Slocum?"

He turned to look back, pulling on the reins to steady his horse. "Ma'am?"

"It's lunchtime."

"Yes, ma'am, it is. Thank you for reminding me."

"Would you like to stay for something to eat?"

Nodding toward the smoke, he said, "Already put my lunch up, ma'am, but thank you anyway."

He turned away again, but Liz called out, "Wait." He turned back, and she was walking toward him. She stopped at the river's edge. Rubbing her hands together, she said, "I . . . I'm sorry. I didn't mean to be . . ." She stopped and looked back at the other three women.

"Rude?" he suggested.

"Thank you," she snapped, "I could have found the word on my own."

"I'm sure."

She turned away, then quickly wheeled back. Holding a hand up, she said, "Let me have my say. I didn't mean to be . . . rude. It's just that . . . that . . ."

"I already told you, Miss Holcom, it's none of my business. We can let it go at that."

Barbara joined Liz at the edge of the river. "Please stay, Mr. Slocum. We have to eat anyway. And . . . suppose those savages come back? Please?"

Slocum shook his head. "Alright. But let me go put out the fire."

"Fine. We'll have everything ready when you get back."

Slocum kicked the roan's flanks, urging the big horse into deep water, and gave it its head to the far shore. He took the opposite bank at a walk, wondering just what the hell was going on. That there was a story, he was certain. That it was unusual, he'd bet the last twenty dollars in his pocket.

He reached the fire a moment later and jumped down just long enough to kick it into smoldering coals. The bird was gone and so was the spit. He poured the last water from his canteen on the coals, walked to the water's edge to refill it, and emptied it again. When the coals stopped hissing, he kicked a little more dirt over the charred branches and refilled his canteen one more time, this time looping it over his saddle horn and remounting.

Heading back upstream, he kept to his own side of the river, as if he thought of the far bank as alien territory, the domain of Liz Holcom, who seemed a formidable opponent, a woman who resented him for no reason he could invent.

When he reached the wagon, he recrossed the river and dismounted alongside the wagon. He tethered the roan to a rear wheel. A tentative puff of smoke rose over the canvas on the far side of the wagon, and Slocum moved around the rear of the wagon. The four women were busily setting out an array of food, dried beef, some cheese and bread. Five small pewter mugs of water sat in a circle at the center of a thick woolen blanket.

Barbara smiled at Slocum. His boots squished as he walked to the blanket, and his pants still dripped water. "We could probably hear you walking a mile away." She laughed.

"I'm used to it," Slocum said. He smiled tightly, conscious that Liz Holcom was as stony-faced as when he'd left. "But I am hungry, and I appreciate this. Thank you all."

"That sounds just a little southern, Mr. Slocum." Barbara looked at him as if she expected him to deny it.

"Yes, ma'am, I guess it is."

"Sit down, Mr. Slocum." Liz Holcom had spoken for the first time since his return.

He curled his legs under him and dropped easily to the ground along the nearest edge of the blanket. "Quite a spread you put on, under the circumstances."

"We tried," Barbara said. "Just help yourself."

Slocum nodded. "Thank you," he said, reaching for a hunk of grainy bread. Before it cleared the plate, Liz rapped the back of his wrist with the wooden handle of a large knife.

"Not yet. Not until we say grace," she barked.

Slocum hadn't heard that tone in a woman's voice since the last day he walked out of school. He mumbled an apology and took off his hat, a split second ahead of Holcom's hand. Bowing his head, he waited for Liz to say something. When she did, he was taken by surprise.

"Go ahead, Mr. Slocum. Say grace."

"Me?"

"You're the man. That is the way it's done, wherever it is you come from, isn't it?"

"Yes'm." Slocum cleared his throat. "You'll have to forgive me, Miss Holcom, but it's been a long time."

"Just go ahead, Mr. Slocum. We're all hungry."

Clearing his throat again, Slocum said, "O Lord, we thank you for these they gifts, and . . . and . . . " He sneaked a peak at Liz, who was watching him with satisfaction. She seemed to be enjoying his discomfort. He'd be damned if he'd let her intimidate him, so he pushed on. ". . . and we ask your blessing on us and ours."

"Amen," Liz added pointedly.

"Amen," Slocum mumbled.

Barbara seemed to be the only one inclined to talk, and she kept up a steady patter while the other three women paid more attention to their meals than to Slocum or to one another. Liz, in particular, seemed withdrawn and angry about something. Slocum was curious, but didn't think he'd get a straight answer, so he didn't bother to ask any questions.

"What brings you out this way, Mr. Slocum?" Barbara asked.

"Nothing particular. I just thought it would be a good place to hook on with an outfit. A man has to work, and Colorado seems like as good a place as any. There's a lot of ranching, and the mines seem to be going full blast. I figured there had to be work out here."

"You don't look like a miner."

"I'm not. But I've run cattle, and there's plenty of spreads could use a man who knows what he's doing. How about you? What brings you out this way?"

"That's no concern of yours, Mr. Slocum."

"Damn it, Liz," Barbara snapped. "The man's just making friendly conversation. Why don't you mind *your* own business. You're not my mother."

"Look," Slocum said, "if you ladies have some secret or something . . . That's fine. I don't mean to pry."

"You're not prying," Barbara said. "I don't want to speak for the others, but I don't mind telling you about myself. I came out here looking for a husband. In fact, I thought I had one."

Slocum seemed confused. "I don't understand," he said.

"You've heard of mail-order brides, haven't you, Mr. Slocum?"

"Yes, ma'am. But begging your pardon, you don't look the type."

"What type is that?" She seemed amused.

"Well, you know. I mean . . ."

"No, I don't. Please enlighten me."

"Well, I always figured a woman must be, well, sort of hard up. Maybe not too pretty or something, you know?"

"What you mean is, you're surprised a woman without a club foot and three eyes would consider such a proposition. Don't you mean that?"

"Well, not exactly, ma'am."

"But almost."

"I guess so. Yes, I guess that is what I was thinking."

"You must realize what a shortage of men there is, Mr. Slocum. Men without a club foot and three eyes are scarce. Since the war, anyway. It's not easy for a woman. And if you want to do something besides cook and raise children, why, it's even more difficult to find a suitable match. Or so I found it, anyway. Unfortunately, I didn't exactly find what I expected on this end, so I was heading back to St. Louis."

"Sorry, I didn't mean anything."

"It's quite alright."

"So what happened? I mean, why didn't it work out?"

Liz interrupted again. "You've told him enough, Barbara."

"Liz, I told you, I was speaking for myself. You don't have to tell Mr. Slocum anything about yourself if you don't want to. There's no rack on his horse, and unless I'm wrong, he has no thumbscrews in his saddlebags. But I'm not ashamed of what happened. It was McDonald who lied, not me."

"Look," Slocum said, "I don't mean to get you ladies all riled up. I was just curious, that's all."

"Never mind her," Barbara said. She took a sip of water, then set the cup down carefully. Without looking up, she continued. "It didn't work out because my situation out here was . . . misrepresented, to say the least."

"You mean he had three eyes, after all?" Slocum laughed, but Barbara didn't join him.

"Nothing that innocent, I'm afraid. No, Mr. Kevin McDonald was a perfectly handsome man. But he had no intention of marrying me. It seems that he is, among other things, the proprietor of a rather unseemly business establishment. He wanted . . ."

"He runs a whorehouse," Liz shouted. "There, are you happy? You know it all now. All you need to know. Are you satisfied?"

Slocum was stunned. "You mean he sent for all four of you ladies, offering to marry each of you?"

Barbara nodded. "And what he really wanted was for us to work for him."

"Christ!" Slocum said, spilling water on his lap in his surprise. "That bastard . . ."

"Actually, not all four of us," Liz put in. "Not me."

Slocum looked at her, waiting for more.

"Liz," Barbara said, "you don't have to say anything."

But Liz brushed the caution aside. And Slocum was even more surprised when she continued. "I worked for him. For two years." She stood up and ran down toward the river.

"I'll go," Mabel said, putting her own plate down. She walked quickly toward Liz Holcom, who stood at the water's edge, her shoulders shaking. But there was no audible evidence of her crying.

Barbara watched Liz for a moment. "We couldn't have made it without her," she said. "She arranged for the wagon and the supplies. From a . . . client. And she got the money together. Saved some and . . . she stole the rest."

"From McDonald?"

Barbara nodded. "Yes. That's why we thought those Indians were after us. I mean, we didn't know they were Indians. We thought McDonald had sent some of his thugs after us. That's why we shot at them."

"So," Slocum said, "you started it. I was wondering about that."

"It was a mistake. We never would have done that if we had known. But McDonald wants his money and . . ."

"And he wants you back. All of you."

"But especially Liz. She's afraid he wants to kill her. I think she's right."

"You ladies are in more trouble than I thought."

Barbara didn't answer right away. When she did, her voice was shaking. "A lot more. Can you help us?"

"Well, I don't know. I don't know what I can do."

"We can pay you. We *will* pay you. Please? You've got to help us."

Slocum chewed thoughtfully on a piece of bread. He swallowed it, gulped down a mouthful of water. Then, instead of answering, he got to his feet. He walked toward the edge of the river. Liz Holcom was still trembling. Mabel watched him for a moment, then stepped aside. Slocum reached out and put a hand on Holcom's shoulder. Without a word, she turned and he wrapped his arms around her.

"It'll be alright," he said.

She kept trembling for a long time. Slocum held her close and stroked her back. While she sobbed into his shoulder, he wondered what he had gotten himself into. And watched the river go by.

4

Liz Holcom took Slocum's hand and tugged him away from the wagon. "I want to talk to you, Mr. Slocum," she said.

When they were out of hearing of the others, she sat on the grass, her back against a tree. Patting the ground beside her, she waited for Slocum to take a seat. Leaning back against the same tree, Slocum sat quietly, waiting for her to gather whatever courage it would take. He didn't want to push, but he thought he knew what was on her mind.

Liz had her knees drawn up, and her palms rubbed relentlessly against the rough denim of her jeans. Except for a faint fluttering of the leaves overhead whenever the wind blew, it was the only sound for a very long time. Slocum tugged a clump of grass out by the roots, shook the dirt free, then tapped the side of his leg with the stiff blades.

"I know what you must think of me, Mr. Slocum," she began. "I . . ."

"Hold it right there, Miss Holcom. You don't owe me any sort of explanation. You don't have to defend yourself to me. People do what they have to do. Whatever it is they do, and whatever the reasons for it, no one has a right to judge them for it. It's a matter between them and their consciences."

"That's very nice of you to say, but I'm afraid it's not that simple. At least, not in my case."

"It never is. But there is still no reason for you to feel you have to defend yourself to me. Not now. Not ever."

"Perhaps not. But I think I ought to. You'll see why in a moment." She reached out and grabbed the grass out of Slocum's hand. "Please don't do that," she said.

"Alright, Miss Holcom. If you feel you have to talk about it, go right ahead. I know it's something easier to talk to a stranger. Sometimes I wish I could do it myself. But I know how hard it is."

"To begin with, you should understand that those girls are different. They're innocent, completely innocent. I can't say that about myself. I suppose I envy them, in a way, but I'm also wise enough to know that that sort of envy is eternal. I can never be like them again, if I ever was. And I'm not talking just about the work I did. It goes deeper than that."

"You don't have to do this, Miss Holcom . . ."

"Yes, Mr. Slocum, I do. Kevin has reason to be angry with me. I stole from him."

"I know."

"No, you don't know. I'm not just talking about the money I took from his safe. I'm talking about all the other times, as well, and other things. In the back of that wagon, there is a metal box, and in that box is ten thousand dollars. Most of it is Kevin's. Most, but not all. I also stole from my clients. Not all of them, and not every time, but often, and over the two years I worked in Sterling, I managed to accumulate quite a bit of money. But it wasn't enough, and so I took more from Kevin."

"He ran a whorehouse. You worked in it. I don't see that you owe him a great deal of loyalty . . . or an apology. What should he expect?"

"As I said, Mr. Slocum, it's not that simple. Before he was my employer, he . . . he was my husband . . ."

"My God! You mean your own husband turned you out, put you to work in a whorehouse?"

"Yes and no. I wasn't new to prostitution. I . . . well, when we met, I was already working. He asked me to marry him, and I said yes. Not because I loved him, and not because he loved me. I don't think either of us really loved the other. But I wanted to get out of New York in the worst way. So did Kevin. So we decided to leave together. It seemed like the thing to do. So did getting married. It was just the most perfect and grand farewell to a life we both despised. That's all there was to it. We were partners of a sort, but not of the sort that husbands and wives usually are.

"When we got to Sterling, things were not exactly what we had expected. We both tried several different jobs, but nothing seemed to work. We were starting to get desperate, but we felt trapped, we had practically no money left. We couldn't have left even if we knew where to go. One thing led to another, and before we knew it, we were back doing the things we knew best."

"So what made you want to give it up?"

"I only went back out of desperation. But I always told myself it was for just a little while. I didn't want to do it forever, just long enough to get the hell out of Sterling. Back to New York, maybe, or out to San Francisco. Kevin refused to let me leave. He didn't know about the money, but I was afraid to leave on my own. I knew he'd try to stop me, that he'd bring me back, so I made a deal with him. We would find a suitable replacement. It was my idea to bring those poor unsuspecting girls out here. But when they arrived, I couldn't go through with it. So . . . here we are."

"And you think you have to apologize for that? Why?"

"Because I lied to those girls. I'm responsible for their being here and I don't think I can get them back where they belong. Not by myself. But the worst part is, they don't even know that I'm responsible. They think I'm a saint or something, their guardian angel . . . their . . ."

"Whore with a heart of gold?" Slocum suggested.

"Alright, yes. But you and I, Mr. Slocum, we know better. We know there's no such thing. So that's why I want to ask you to do something."

"What is it?"

"I want you to help me get these girls on a train back East. I can't do it alone, and I'm afraid for them. If Kevin does catch us, and I know he will try, I don't know what might happen. I'll pay you, of course. I'm not asking you to be a good Samaritan. There are no more saints, Mr. Slocum, I know that. If there ever were. And I don't expect you to be one. All I ask is that you help me get the girls to Denver. From there, I can get them to St. Louis.

The rest will be up to them. But they should have that chance, and I mean to see they do."

"I don't know, Miss Holcom. I . . ."

"Five hundred dollars, Mr. Slocum. I'll pay you five hundred dollars. One hundred upfront, and the balance when the train leaves. Think about it. It's an awful lot of money."

"Miss Holcom, I'm no bodyguard. I . . ."

"One thousand, Mr. Slocum. That's my final offer. Take it or leave it."

Slocum chewed on the inside of his cheek for a while. He could think of a hundred reasons not to accept the offer. It was short-term. It was high risk. Riding herd on four women had all the potential of turning into a nightmare. On the other hand, he could think of a thousand reasons to accept. He looked at Liz Holcom for a moment, then reached out and snatched the clump of grass still dangling from her fingers.

"If I accept your offer, you do what I say, when I say it. The same goes for the others. I don't want to debate anything, not with any of you."

"Fair enough."

"You got any other secrets I should know, I want to hear them now. I don't want any surprises."

"No secrets. None at all."

Slocum reached out and tapped her on the nose with the dried grass. "You got a deal, Miss Holcom."

"Just one thing, Mr. Slocum."

"What's that?"

"You don't tell the girls about my part in getting them out here. You do, and I'll kill you. I don't care whether I have to shoot you in the back or sneak up in the dark and slit your throat. I will find a way, and I will do it."

"Agreed."

"And these girls go back to St. Louis in the same condition in which they arrived. You keep your hands to yourself. Understood?"

Slocum nodded. He got to his feet and walked down to the water's edge. He knelt down and leaned forward to take a long, slow drink of the cold, clear water. When he was no longer thirsty, he stuck his head under the water and shook it from side to side, then brushed his soaking wet hair back with his fingers.

As he started to get up, he saw Liz Holcom's reflection in the water. She was standing right beside him when he got to his feet. "One other thing," she said.

Slocum sighed. "What is it now?"

"Don't tell them I'm paying you. As far as they're concerned, the charity is yours, not mine."

"Why?"

"Never mind. Do you accept the condition?"

"Miss Holcom, for a thousand dollars, I'll tell them anything you want."

"There are all kinds of whores, aren't there, Mr. Slocum."

"Yes, ma'am. That's the Liz I've grown to love."

She glared at him, then turned on her heel and marched back toward the wagon. By the time he caught up to her, she had already told the others about their arrangement.

"Alright, ladies. We have our work cut out for us. It's a hundred and fifty miles to Denver. If we're lucky, we can make thirty miles a day in the wagon. If not, well . . ." He shrugged. "But there are a number of things we have to get straight. Rule number one: No shooting at Indians or anybody else, no matter who you think they are, unless I say so. Rule number two: If I countermand rule number one, by all means, please make sure you hit somebody. Don't waste ammunition. We'll be following the South Platte at least half the way. We are liable to run into anything from Cheyenne to grizzly bears. If we do, we are going to need every bullet we've got, if not more."

"That's it? Those are the only rules?" Barbara McDonough was grinning at him.

"For now, yes. There will no doubt be a need for others. I'll advise you when the time comes. And I'm sure it will. But I want you all to understand one thing: Do what I say as soon as I say it. Any hesitation can get us all killed. If Miss Holcom is right about McDonald, we *will* be followed. I have no idea by how many men, so we have to prepare for the worst and hope for the best. Any questions?"

"Just one," Barbara said, still grinning.

"Shoot."

"Why are you doing this?"

"Liz, here, reminds me of my grandma." He glanced at Holcom who returned a glare hot enough to peel paint off a barn door. "If that's it, let's get this stuff back in the wagon and head out. Make sure we have plenty of water. If not, get it now. I don't want to stop before nightfall, unless it's absolutely necessary."

Fifteen minutes later, they were ready to roll. Slocum helped the women into the wagon, then raised the tailgate and slammed the retaining pins through the rusty rings. As before, Liz Holcom, her red hair once again hidden under the battered straw hat, was in the driver's seat.

Slocum couldn't decide whether it was better to ride ahead of the wagon or to protect its rear. Either way was risky, but there was no way to do both, so he split his time more or less evenly, riding ahead now and then for a quarter mile or so to check the terrain ahead, then dropping back to hang behind the wagon, checking over his shoulder frequently and wondering when, and if, McDonald and his men would put in an appearance.

He couldn't shake the suspicion that Liz Holcom had not told him everything. But he couldn't even guess what she might be hiding, or why. In the long run, he knew it didn't really matter. What was done was done. He'd made his choice, and he would have to live up to it. He only hoped Liz was wrong about her ex-husband. But there wasn't a thing he could do, even about that.

To get his mind off his suspicions, he kept remembering the mocking look in Barbara McDonough's eyes. They had gone more than ten miles before he realized that might be even more dangerous than anything Liz might have kept from him.

It was going to be an interesting week.

5

The Rockies towered far ahead, and Slocum was concerned about sunset. He wanted to establish a campsite before it got too dark, but defending four women who were not afraid of guns was not the same as defending a campsite with four women who themselves could shoot. If they were attacked, his gun would be the one that mattered. The rest would keep the attackers honest, maybe. But only for a while, maybe. If they were lucky.

He was a quarter of a mile ahead of the wagon now, on a low ridge. Looking back down the trail, he could see the sluggish contraption rocking over the uneven ground. In the predusk quiet, he could hear it squeak and squeal with every twist of the wagon bed. He waited patiently for the lumbering team to haul their load up the winding trail.

When the wagon reached the ridge line, Liz Holcom reined in her team. "Anything wrong?" she asked.

"Not yet," Slocum said. "But I think we better stop for the night as soon as we find a suitable place. We'll want water, but we'll also want to have some cover." He pointed downslope into the next valley. A narrow band of trees coiled across the valley floor. "I don't see any water, but there's probably a creek in there somewhere. They'll expect us to stick to the river, so if we stay inland a mile or so, we give ourselves a little extra advantage."

"Sounds sensible to me, Mr. Slocum." Liz had reverted to the flat, emotionless tone she had used in the beginning. Slocum wondered what she was hiding, and from whom.

"Alright then. Let's take the trail halfway down, then when the land levels off a bit, down by that stand of pines, we'll cut over to the left. Even if the going is a little rough,

I think the wagon can make it. I'll stay far enough ahead to check it out."

The canvas behind Liz rustled, then Barbara stuck her head out. "Anything wrong?" she asked.

"No," Liz snapped before Slocum could say anything. "It's alright."

Slocum kneed his mount into the descent, and the big roan picked its way carefully over the loose stone littering the trail. The stand of pines he'd mentioned was no more than fifteen or twenty feet off the trail, and beyond it the ground looked to be fairly flat. No noticeable dips disturbed the smooth surface of the tall grass. And he couldn't see any outcroppings of rock large enough to impede the wagon.

The wagon followed about fifty yards behind him. Twice, he had to change course to avoid an obstacle that might have proven too tough for the exhausted team or too hard on the rickety wagon itself. But he had guessed right. A small stream wound across the valley floor, on the far side of the tree line. He headed south a quarter mile until he found a shallow depression where the stream spread out into a small pond. The trees were thick enough to hide the wagon.

They settled for a bare bones campsite. The women took nothing out of the wagon except for bedrolls. Slocum built a small cook fire, scouring along the stream bank for the driest wood he could find to keep the smoke down. They could have gone without a fire altogether for their meals, but they would still need one for later, when it got cold.

While the women tended the small fire, Slocum went out into the grass and rigged a few small snares. With any luck, he might catch two or three rabbits. A little fresh meat would be good for all of them. He asked Karen to go with him. She seemed reluctant at first, until he explained that someone would have to check the snares before he got back.

"Back? Where are you going?" she asked.

"Don't worry about it. I just want to scout the trail behind us a mile or so." She seemed relieved and followed him up into the thick grass. He worked quickly as the sun began to hint at changing color. It was only four o'clock, and they still had a good three hours of daylight, but he wanted everyone close to camp by sundown, including himself.

Working with some green switches from a cottonwood and some sturdy twine from the wagon, he managed to set five simple snares. Karen watched him quietly.

When the last of the snares was set, she said, "Now, what do I do if you catch something?"

"All you have to do is grab hold of the little bugger and twist its head around. That'll break his neck. Bring anything we catch on back to the camp."

"Do rabbits bite?"

"They might, if they're scared enough. But usually they freeze up and go limp, playing dead. If you work fast, you don't have anything to worry about. Can you do that?"

"I think so," she said. She wasn't convinced, and neither was he.

"Maybe you should take Barbara with you. Wait about an hour though. You go tramping around too soon, you might scare off a catch or two."

They walked downhill to the wagon. Karen kept looking over her shoulder, as if she still didn't know what she was supposed to do. Slocum looked at her for a moment, then patted her arm. She smiled for the first time that day.

The severity of her hair, pulled back into a tight bun, and the absence of makeup had fooled him. She just might be the prettiest of the bunch, he thought. Taller than the others, she had muscular legs and small breasts, giving her a girlish look, more like a filly than a mare. But in profile, the even features, smooth white skin, and pale pink lips reminded him of a cameo his mother had worn on special occasions. He returned the smile, and she seemed to relax a little. "You'll do fine," he said as he mounted up.

"Where are you going?" Liz demanded, rushing toward him.

"If you're right that we might be followed, it wouldn't hurt to take a look. I thought I'd ride back up trail a couple of miles, see if I spot anything. That next to last ridge we crossed should give me a pretty good look at the last few miles."

"I thought you were going to stay with us."

"I'm not leaving, Miss Holcom. But the last thing we need is a surprise visit in the middle of the night. I'm supposed to do a job for you, and I will, but I already told you to keep your mouth shut. If you remember, you agreed to that."

"I remember. I'm sorry, I'm just a little scared, I guess. You have no idea what that man is like when he's angry."

"No, I don't. But if he doesn't catch us, it doesn't much matter, does it? I'd rather run like hell than have to fight like hell. If we're careful and smart, we'll make it without any trouble."

The other women watched the exchange carefully, as if they were trying to catch familiar words in a foreign language.

"Be careful, Mr. Slocum," Barbara shouted. "We're all getting fond of you."

"Speak for yourself," Liz barked.

Slocum struggled to keep from smiling as he rode off. He was beginning to be fond of them, too. Even Liz Holcom, who seemed like a coiled spring uncertain of which way it ought to snap. As he rode back up the second ridge, higher than anything they'd crossed, and higher than anything in front of them for a good twenty miles, he wondered what he ought to be looking for.

A search party could consist of two men or twenty. Liz didn't seem to know and Slocum couldn't guess. In all probability, McDonald would have at least one man out front, scouting the most likely route. He might even have three or four scouts out in front of a large party. But if a scout stumbled on them, they would have some time to get ready. If it was a breakneck, all-out pursuit, though, they wouldn't have the luxury.

Just below the top of the ridge, Slocum dismounted and tethered his horse to a slab of broken stone. He lay on the ground and squirmed forward just far enough to be able to look down the other side. He pulled binoculars out of a worn leather case and tracked back down the trail, starting right in front of him and following the twists and turns all the way to the valley floor. Nothing moved along the trail, and Slocum let his breath out a little more easily.

He worked his way back up the far side of the valley, more slowly now, and still saw nothing moving but the grass. He watched the line of the opposite ridge for a couple of minutes, looking for anything, a trace of smoke, a plume of dust, a bird exploding into the sky, anything that might tell him someone was on their tails. A single horseman, especially one who knew how to be careful, would not betray himself that way, but at least he knew they weren't being closely followed by a large party.

Slocum crawled backward down the slope until he could stand without breaking the ridge line. When he got to his feet, he looked once more at the sky through the glasses. It was empty of anything but a few clouds, and even they seemed to be stationary. They were starting to turn pink, and his shadow splashed some distance up the hill as the sun had started to slip.

He climbed into the saddle and tucked the glasses into their case. He draped the strap over his saddle horn and eased the horse into a walk. Over the next ridge, he could see just a little smear of smoke from his fire. It wasn't much, but it would be enough for an experienced tracker to want to check out. He wished they could do without it, but even late summer nights in the foothills were prone to be cold. The women, with the possible exception of Liz, were probably not used to the outdoors, but he would try to convince them to go without a fire during the night.

When he reached the wagon, Karen rushed over to greet him. She held three big jack rabbits by the hind legs. "Look what we caught," she said, almost jumping up and down in her surprised pleasure. "Three of them. What do we do now?"

Barbara said, "I wanted to skin them, but she wouldn't let me. She said it's up to Mr. Slocum." She laughed, and Karen pouted.

"I'll take care of it," he said, slipping off the roan and patting its flanks. He took the three rabbits and handed the reins to Karen. "Just tie him up. I'll handle him when I'm finished with these."

Slocum walked into the trees and dropped the rabbits on the ground by the edge of the stream. He worked quickly, skinning them without regard to the pelts, which were of no use. He wanted to get the meat on the fire as soon as possible. By the time he started on the third, he heard footsteps. He glanced over his shoulder to see Karen watching him. Her pout was still there. "Barbara was right," she said. "Darn it."

Slocum laughed in spite of himself, but Karen didn't seem to mind. She was too distressed at having been outguessed by Barbara. When the last rabbit had been skinned and gutted, Slocum dragged all three of them through the cold water to rinse them, then hauled them back, still dripping, to the camp. He spitted all three and showed Karen how to turn them to cook them quickly and evenly.

The meal went quickly. The women seemed too tired to talk, and Slocum wanted to get the fire out as soon as he could. When he finished gnawing on his last piece of meat, he said, "Can you ladies get through the night without the fire?"

"Why?" Naturally, it was Liz who wanted to know. "Are we being followed? Did you see someone?"

"No. But the less help we give them, the better off we'll be. The firelight might give us away after sundown." He looked up at the sky, now almost purple. In fifteen minutes, it would be black. "I thought maybe you all could sleep in the wagon."

"What about you?" Barbara asked. "Where will you sleep?"

Slocum jerked a thumb back uphill. "Up there," he said. "I'd kind of like to keep an ear peeled. From up there, I can hear them coming up the other side of the hill. If they're there, that is."

"Well," Karen said, "we all agreed that you were in charge. If you think we should sleep in the wagon, then I do too." The others nodded their agreement.

"Alright then, let's kill this fire," Slocum said. He stood up and started kicking dirt on it while the women gathered their bedrolls and shoved them back into the wagon. When the fire was covered, Slocum walked over to Liz Holcom. "I know it might be cramped in there, but I think it's best."

"I'm not arguing, Mr. Slocum."

"I know, but I just wanted you to understand that I'm not trying to make things any harder than they have to be. I just think we should be careful."

She nodded without looking at him, then closed the canvas cover after Mabel climbed in. She grabbed her own bedroll and walked around to the front of the wagon. "I'll sleep on the seat," she said. "It's too crowded for all four of us inside."

"Look, you need me, you hear something, whatever. I'll be up under that stand of pines."

"We'll be fine, Mr. Slocum. Don't worry yourself."

6

Slocum lay on his back, on top of his bedroll. Too restless
to sleep, he watched the stars and listened to the sounds of
the night. Every now and then, a shooting star would spurt
out of nowhere, burning itself into his vision for just a little
longer than its flight. Far below him, somewhere among
the trees, an owl argued with the silence. The bird sounded
as if it were angry. The ghostly placidity of the cry was
missing, replaced by a burr-edged hoot, sharp as a buzz
saw.

His legs were crossed, and he tapped the toe of one boot
against the sole of the other. The crickets seemed to pick
up the same rhythm, blending in with the hollow taps. He
wondered whether it was he or the crickets that took the
lead. In the far distance, a wolf howled and was answered
by another, even farther away.

Slocum wondered why everyone seemed to think of the
night as dead time, a time when nothing moved, and when
nothing happened that mattered. While he lay there on the
hillside, predator and prey were both abroad, playing out
their pageant in the darkness. Bats were eating bugs, owls
were chasing mice, and wolves were stalking deer and
pronghorn. And in another shadow play, Kevin McDonald
stalked four women who meant him no harm at all.

Restless and on edge, Slocum sat up, wrapping his arms
around his knees. He rocked back and forth on the base of
his spine, as if he were a child with no one to put him to
sleep. It was chilly and getting colder by the minute. The
wind picked up and rustled the branches of the pine trees to
his left. The stiff branches cracked against one another, the
huge trunks creaked with the stress of their swaying, and

brittle needles hissed as they rained down through lower limbs and on into the grass.

He needed rest and he knew it. He lay down again, this time on his stomach. Crossing his arms, he turned his head and propped one cheek on the pillow of his forearms. He tugged the bedroll in around him and closed his eyes, hoping that intention would this one time be the mother of necessity. But his nerves still fired, responding to every creak of the trees, every flutter of night wings high overhead.

When the twig snapped, Slocum froze. He wasn't sure where the sound had come from. Looking back up the hill, he half expected to see a silhouette outlined against the sky, some amorphous shape defining itself as it moved across the stars behind it. But he saw nothing. Moving his right arm as quietly as possible, he reached for the Colt Navy pistol on his hip. He held his breath as it cleared the holster, the front sight scratching against the leather.

Then he heard a footstep. He muffled the hammer with his left hand and cocked it. He started to roll to his left when he heard his name.

"Slocum? Are you awake? Slocum?" It was a woman's voice, but the sibilant whisper obscured her identity. "Slocum?" This time it was a little louder.

"Miss Holcom? Is that you?" More footsteps, this time moving toward him as he sat up. He still held the pistol in his hand, but released the hammer with a click. The footsteps stopped as suddenly as they had begun.

"What was that noise?" Liz asked.

"Nothing, never mind. Are you alright?"

"I'm alright. I just couldn't sleep. I was hoping you were still awake. I'm not disturbing you, am I?"

"Sit down," Slocum whispered.

The footsteps resumed. He could see her now, moving gingerly up the path. As she drew closer, she walked even faster, like a kid approaching home after dark. She nearly tripped over his outstretched legs, and he reached out to catch her. She gave a start, then laughed. "I didn't even see you," she said.

Slocum realized she had brought her bedroll along, cradled in her arms like an infant. She dropped the roll and leaned over to spread the blanket out. She knelt at the far edge and smoothed it with her hand. Finding something underneath, she flipped a corner up and groped in the grass until she found it again and tossed the stone off into the grass.

Satisfied, she sat on the blanket and pulled the lower half over her legs. "The wagon seat was too short for me, and too hard for me to get comfortable. You don't mind, do you? I couldn't bear the thought of sleeping alone on the ground down there."

"No, I don't mind. But aren't you afraid of what the other women might think?"

She laughed. "They already know I was . . . am . . . a whore. What difference does it make what they think?"

"How about me," Slocum said. "I have a reputation, too, you know."

She smacked him. He hadn't expected it. His left ear rang and his cheek felt as if it had been seared with a branding iron. In his mind's eye, he could see the outline of her fingers glowing on his skin.

"I'm sorry," she said. "I shouldn't have done that."

"No, you shouldn't have," he said. "That hurt like hell."

He felt her hand on his cheek again, this time probing with cool fingers. "I . . ."

"Don't say anything," Slocum said. "I should watch what I say. I'm sorry."

"No, I guess I was just angry because you were right. I'm just so used to . . . I don't know what."

"Forget it," he said. He lay back on the bedroll and flapped the blanket over his legs. He folded his arms behind his head and lay there, his face turned away from her. For a long time, he listened to the sound of her breathing. She sat up once, and he thought she was going to leave. But she just rearranged the blanket. The steady hiss of her breath was almost drowned out by the sound of flesh on cloth. He wanted to say something, but didn't know what it should be. It just seemed that theirs was one of those rare meetings of two people who cannot understand one another at all. Locked in permanent offense, neither could seem to find a way to some sort of armed neutrality.

She finally stopped fussing with the blanket and he thought she would at last go to sleep. Instead, she leaned over him, her hair brushing his cheek. He lay rigid as a stone, not knowing what to expect, fearful that if he did anything at all it was certain to be the wrong thing. He had given up trying to read her moods. Her intentions were a perfect puzzle.

When lips grazed his cheek, he shivered. He felt her breath hot on his ear. Her hand lay flat on his stomach for a long moment, then she kissed his cheek again, this time sliding her lips across to find his. He lay still, uncertain whether to respond and, if so, how. But her lips were insistent, the tip of her tongue probing until he relaxed enough to let it slide into his mouth like liquid fire.

He wanted to respond more actively, but Liz seemed to know what she wanted, and until he had at least a faint idea, he thought it best to react. Her hand slid to the buttons on his shirt and undid a pair of them, just enough to allow her to slip it inside and touch his skin. Her fingers moved in slow circles, teasing the hair on his chest for a moment, then fumbling at another button. This time she opened the shirt all the way, she moved her head lower, letting her lips slide down his throat and across his chest. The air was cold, and he could feel the pebbled texture getting slick as she licked his skin. Her hair smelled like flowers of some kind, while wave after wave of the dark red rose and fell, breaking over him like ocean swells.

And he decided it was time for him to do something. He let his hand rest on her back and was surprised to feel nothing but smooth, cool skin. He realized it had not after all been the blanket she had worried over. He let his palm stay flat against her back, and he lay there feeling the play of muscles under the satiny skin as she continued to tease him, sliding her tongue from his navel to his throat and back again. She paused once to tug at a tuft of chest hair with her teeth.

He let his hand slide lower on her back. At the curve of her hip, he realized she had taken off more than her shirt.

He slipped lower, taking the fullness of her ass in one hand, smooth as marble and cold as ice. He teased the cleft between her cheeks with a fingertip, and she wiggled, but did nothing to stop him.

She was after his belt now. Pausing just long enough to unbuckle it and pull it open, she went back to nuzzling his belly while one practiced hand undid the buttons of his fly. She was on her knees and Slocum raised his hips to let her tug the dungarees down around his ankles. She turned to him then, and he could see a distant, almost frozen smile as she bent over him. He felt himself stiffen and worked to get his boots off with no success.

She reached out with one hand and ran a long sharp fingernail the length of his shaft. He felt himself grow even harder, then her hand closed around it. Slowly, she began to caress him, long slow strokes, stopping at the tip and at the base, letting his memory supply one stroke for every one of hers. He strained upward and she worked a little faster, then leaned over to curl her tongue around him for just a second.

She straightened and brought one leg over, then lowered herself, one knee on either side of him. He strained harder, but could not reach her. He reached for her, letting his hands rest on her hips. He tried to pull her down, but she fought against him. Slocum let his hands slip up along her sides, stopping for a moment at every rib, until he found her breasts. He cupped them gently, letting his thumbs trace small circles around each nipple.

She leaned closer, and he felt her hair sweep across his chest, then a breast brush his lips. He opened and sucked the nipple in, letting his tongue tickle the stiff button, then opening wide and sucking his mouth full of the cool, smooth flesh of her. She teased him, backing away until he followed, his teeth tugging on the nipple, then leaning forward again, filling his mouth again.

She pulled free, then offered him the other breast, and he dug his fingers into the cheeks of her ass, kneading the firm flesh, shaping it, like a sculptor working with the perfect clay. She teased him now, letting the moist tendrils of her bush tickle the tip of his cock. She let her body sink toward him until he felt her lips close over him. He thrust upward and sank the head of his shaft in her but she backed away, letting it slip free. He felt her juice trickle down his rod, cold in the night air, and then she reached for him again, letting him in out of the cold.

She started to fall toward him and he steeled himself for the abrupt and sudden withdrawal, but this time she fooled him, sliding all the way down until he was buried full length in her. He felt a ripple as her muscles stroked him and then she started to rise and fall. She rode up until he was sure he would slip free, the wind swirling around him, making him shiver, and then slowly, deliberately, she wrapped him in the hot, wet center of her, plummeting all the way down. She rose again, and fell again. Then faster, then again, faster still.

She was breathing in short, sharp gasps and he could feel his heart hammering against his ribs. Up she slid, and down, clutching him tightly, then letting him go. He felt the trickle of hot juices on his thighs as he strained upward to meet her, then backed away. Faster and faster they moved, in perfect harmony now, and she started to cry out, her voice deep and rich, an animal growl from somewhere deep inside of her. And he tried to reach that depth himself as he drove harder and deeper.

And he could hold on no longer. He raised his hips and held her, impaled on the full length of him. He held her by the hips, pressing her down as the final spasm surged through him. She sighed and fell forward on his chest as he let go completely, and he lay there, drained, his muscles quivering like jelly, and listened to the sound of his own desperate breathing.

She wriggled her hips, her breasts flattened between them, their mingled sweat letting her slide as if they had both been oiled. He thought for a moment she was just trying to get comfortable.

Until her lips found his ear. "That's just to make sure you leave the girls alone. Don't think it means anything to me." Then she rolled off him so quickly and so completely, he wondered whether she had been there at all.

7

At sunup, Slocum had already been awake for an hour. Liz was gone. He glanced at the ground where her bedroll had been. Even the grass had rebounded, leaving barely a trace that she had ever been there. He was already dressed, and he made up his kit with the mindless ease that comes only from long practice.

He wanted to get moving, but was reluctant to face Liz too soon. She had kept him so far off balance, he felt like a schoolboy. And he was mad as hell. She had played him like a cheap piano, all clanks and rusty springs. Rather than ride down, he saddled the roan and started downhill on foot, pulling the horse behind him. He was halfway there when the first shot exploded below.

Slocum scrambled into the saddle and started toward the wagon. Something slammed into his thigh, then he heard the crack of a rifle. He felt the blood soaking his dungarees and trickling down between the denim and his calf. His boot began to fill with blood, and he squeezed the wound. It was superficial, but he was bleeding heavily where the slug had plowed through the thick flesh of his thigh.

He dug his spurs into the stallion's flanks, and the horse spurted forward, its long downhill strides sending hammer blows up his spine. He saw a thin wisp of gray smoke and cursed himself for being so careless. The women must have started a fire despite his injunction.

He heard no more gunshots, but the smoke was getting thicker by the second. It was no campfire, that was for sure. Slocum was getting light-headed as he continued to bleed. The pressure of his hand wasn't good enough to stem the flow, but there was no time to bind it. That would have to wait until . . . what? He realized with a shock that he didn't know.

The horse fought the reins now, running out of terror and out of control. Slocum felt himself slipping from the saddle. Everything went yellow, then white. Tiny balls of light swirled before his eyes and he felt himself falling. He reached for the saddle horn, felt it slip away from his fingers, and then he lost his balance altogether. His head hit the ground hard, sending another tidal wave of light across his field of vision. As it started to go completely black, he knew he was losing consciousness, only dimly aware that his left leg, the wounded leg, was caught in the stirrup.

He was aware of the pain first. He heard ringing in his ears and tried to open his eyes. The sun beat down on him, and he could feel its heat on his skin. His eyelids were red where the sun washed over his face. They seemed stuck together with something, but he didn't think it was blood. The pain was all in his leg and back. He brushed the lids with his fingers, felt a crust that crumbled under the pressure, and pushed it away. His lids fluttered now, and he pried them open one by one with a pair of fingers.

Slocum could see now, but was almost sorry. His left leg was a mess. The boot was gone, and the leg of his dungarees was stiff with blood. He tried to sit up, but the movement sent searing flames across his back and shoulders. He rolled on his stomach, careful to keep pressure off the throbbing thigh. He felt the heat on his back now and realized his shirt had been torn to shreds. He remembered dangling from the stirrup just before he passed out.

Looking back up the hill, he could see the flattened grass where he had been dragged by the frightened roan. A swath of a hundred, maybe a hundred and fifty feet. Thank God it wasn't any farther, he thought. Keeping the left leg out straight, he tried to raise himself to his right knee. He ignored the pain in his ravaged back and managed to brace himself with both arms.

Balanced on one knee, gingerly, he tried to bend the

wounded leg, careful not to flex it too quickly. He didn't want the congealed blood to tear away from the wound and start the bleeding all over again, but he had to get up. He had to find the women, and he had to find his horse. In what order, he wasn't sure.

All he knew for certain was that he had to do something now, as soon as he could, the sooner the better. To do anything at all would prove that he hadn't been beaten, that he was down, but not out. Slocum managed to get to his right foot, then swung the left leg forward stiffly. He tried his weight on it, and it seemed to hold as long as he used it primarily for balance. He ripped the remains of his shirt off. The front and the sleeves were largely intact, but the back had been shredded beyond recognition.

Tearing the sleeves loose, Slocum rolled the remains in a ball and threw them away in disgust. He rolled the sleeves lengthwise, knotted them together, then bound them around his wounded thigh. The pressure sent a wave of pain through the leg, and he felt nauseous for a moment. He swallowed hard, then pulled the binding a little tighter and knotted it securely.

He tried the leg again. It would take a little weight, but not much. Even the gentle slope was going to present problems. He had to put most of his weight on the good leg, drag the wounded one after it, not too difficult to do on level ground. But on a descent, even a shallow one, it wasn't possible to protect the injury nearly as well. He looked around for something he could use as a cane, or a crutch, but there was nothing but grass for as far as he could see in any direction. He could crawl, of course, but he refused to consider that as an option.

He started to hobble, gritting his teeth with every tentative step. Heading toward the trees, still some two hundred and fifty yards below, he noticed that a pall of black smoke had flattened out and hung just above the treetops. He remembered thinking the women had built a fire, then dismissing it when the smoke got thicker.

He didn't want to consider the alternative. After fifty yards, he tried a new gambit, moving sidewise, good leg on the downhill side, and that worked a little better as long as he let the right leg take the bulk of his weight. He kept an eye out for the horse, but so far had seen not a trace of the big roan. He had seen no motion at all since regaining consciousness.

High overhead, a hawk cried out, and he looked up at the bright sky, laced with thin wisps of clouds, for a moment. He felt very small and very vulnerable. His pistol was gone, probably lying in the grass somewhere upslope, but he couldn't afford to waste time looking for it. He had to attend to his leg first. He had to wash the wound and try to fashion some sort of support for walking.

And he had to find his other boot. It had probably traveled a bit with the horse after his leg pulled free, but it could be anywhere between the spot where he awoke and the horse, wherever the hell he was now. But it could have been worse, and he knew it. His ankle could have been broken. Despite that apparent stroke of good luck, it was still bad enough that the thought didn't make him feel better. He didn't see that he had much to be thankful for.

Except, perhaps, the lousy marksmanship of whoever had shot at him. And he was lucky, too, that the horse had not been killed. His chances alone and on foot would have been less than slim, much closer to none than he cared to consider. Fifteen yards farther on, he spotted something off to the left a little. It was a depression in the tall grass. He bit his lower lip and changed course.

He could look down into the depression when still a few yards away. At the bottom of the grass bowl, lying on its side, lay his other boot. He felt like shouting, and then wondered why so simple a thing could mean so much.

He bent over carefully to retrieve the boot, then resumed his painful descent. The ground was starting to level out, and the going was easier. He reached the first line of undergrowth and had to turn sideways to push through with his good leg. He worked his way back toward the campsite, and the closer he got, the stronger the smell of charred wood.

Pushing out of the scrub and into the small clearing, he could see the wagon, its iron hoops no longer supporting the canvas cover. The metal was blackened and the wooden sides were charred. Slocum hobbled toward it, forgetting about his leg for a second, until the first stride reminded him.

About the only part of the wagon untouched by the flames was the tongue. The team, tied to a tree nearby, both lay on the ground. Slocum heard the intense hum of insects, and as he got closer he saw the swarm of flies around the animals' heads. He bent over to pick up a rock and hit one of the horses on the flank. The stone landed with the dull sound of wood on wood. The flies hummed louder, and he realized both animals were dead. That explained at least two of the gunshots he remembered.

Shaking his head in despair, Slocum pushed on through the trees and down to the water. He lowered himself to the weedy sand and unbuckled his belt. He untied the makeshift binding, pulling it away carefully from the wound. With a pocket knife, he sawed at the dungarees, cutting the left leg off above the wound. Working cautiously, he tugged the pants down over the severed leg and lowered himself into the water. The cold sent a shiver through him, but it numbed the pain a little. He lay back, letting the frigid water curl around the cuts and scrapes across his shoulders.

Slocum lay there on the streambed, shivering in the cold for a few minutes, then rubbed himself all over, trying to wash off the clotted blood and smeared dirt. He ducked his head under, combed his hair with his fingers to get rid of the weeds and burrs tangled in it, then tossed his head to shake off the water. He got to his feet, feeling vaguely ridiculous in his soaking underpants.

He hobbled back to the bank and sat on a patch of grass. With painstaking caution, he worked the pant leg loose, wincing every time the cloth tugged at the long scab over the wound. The coagulated blood had softened considerably in the water, and he managed to get the cloth away with only a little new bleeding.

Grabbing the knotted sleeves, Slocum bound them tightly around the three-inch furrow plowed through the meaty part of his leg. Knotting the cloth again, he reached for his pants and slipped them back on, ignoring the wet underwear. Movement was easier now, but his back stung in a hundred places. He could feel every scrape and tear with his fingers, and turned his back to the stream, using it as a mirror. Even in the undulating surface of a pool, he could see the angry red welts, and he wished he had something to dress them. Hell, he wished he had something to dress himself.

Hobbling to the wagon, he peered over the charcoaled sides of the bed. A tumbled mess of ashes and smoke-blackened cloth covered everything, but it looked as if only the outside of the wagon had burned, as if it had been doused with some volatile liquid that burned off quickly, before the wood really got going.

He cut a branch from a nearby tree and combed through the ashes with it. Under the remains of a badly charred blanket, he found the top of a wooden trunk, three straps of brass glittering in the ashen heap. He leaned over the side of the wagon and grabbed for one end of the trunk. His fingers closed over a metal handle, and he tugged, putting all his weight into it. Fierce pain flamed through his wounded thigh, but he ignored it as the trunk began to rise a little. Something shifted with a grating scrape, and one end of the trunk came up. He was able to pull it toward him, now.

He hoisted the free end of the trunk onto the ruined sideboards, then started to pull it all the way free.

"Slocum?" the voice asked.

He turned to see Barbara McDonough racing toward him. He reached out to catch her as she collapsed in his arms.

"Thank God it's you," she said. "I was so frightened."

"What happened?" Slocum asked, stroking her hair to calm her down.

"I'm not sure. I was down by the water getting washed. I heard gunshots, and I hid." She was blubbering, and he could barely understand her. "I could hear men talking. I didn't want them to see me."

"They must have kidnapped the others," Slocum said.

"I was afraid they..."

"No, it was the horses they shot."

"Oh, thank God. I thought . . . of, I don't know what I thought. I just . . ." She shook her head. "What are we going to do?"

"Now just settle down, Barbara. We'll find them. And we'll get them back. But we'll have to hurry. We have a lot to do. We need to find my horse and my gun. I need some clothes."

She noticed his leg for the first time. "Oh, you're hurt."

"It's alright. Look, help me with this trunk. There's got to be something I can wear here somewhere."

"That's my trunk," she said. "I'm sure there must be something."

But Slocum was already thinking about what they'd need that wouldn't be in her trunk.

8

Slocum shrugged into the shirt. It was snug, but it would have to do.

"What about the pants?" Barbara asked. "You can't wear those. It gets too cold at night."

"Look, I can manage with a shirt that nearly cuts off my circulation. But there's no way in hell I can get into a pair of your pants."

"Who said anything about mine? Wait a minute." She leaned over the trunk and rummaged through a mound of neatly folded clothing. Near the bottom of the pile, she found what she was looking for. Tugging it loose, she hauled a pair of dungarees out and handed them to Slocum. "Try these."

Slocum held them up to his waist. They were a little long, but he could roll the cuffs. The waist was a little larger than he usually wore, but they would be more than serviceable. He hobbled into the trees and changed, hobbling back with the cuffs bunched around his ankles.

"Here," Barbara said, "let me fix those." She knelt in front of him, then quickly rolled the excess material into two neat, flat cuffs. "Back up a second," she said, placing a hand on his stomach and pushing him away. He took two steps back, and she smiled. "They look fine," she said.

"Thanks," Slocum said.

"You're welcome."

"Do you mind if I ask a question?"

"Of course not."

"Why do you have these pants in the first place?"

"They're not mine, if that's what you're wondering. They were my husband's."

"Oh . . ."

"Don't worry about it. He's . . . well, let's just let it go at that, shall we?"

"I didn't know you were married," Slocum said.

"I said, let's let it go, alright?" She turned away and got to her feet. Her back was arched and her head down. Slocum started to move toward her, but she heard his feet on the sand and moved away slowly, knowing she could outrun him if she had to.

"Are you alright?" he asked.

"I just need to be alone for a minute, okay?" She walked into the trees, leaving Slocum with his mouth open, wondering what he had done wrong.

"Don't be long, alright? I'll be ready to look for the horse in a couple of minutes. As soon as we find him, I want to get going. They already have a couple of hours head start on us." But she said nothing, and he wondered whether she had heard him, or, if she had, whether she had understood him.

While he waited for her to regain her composure, he took a quick inventory of the wagon. Three more trunks and several smaller packages, all smothered in ashes, lay in the ruined wagon bed. Slocum hauled them to the end and lifted them down one by one, sliding each in under the wagon.

In a far corner, he saw a small metal box and pulled it free of the debris. It was locked, and he shook it. It sounded as if it were full of paper. A second one, just like it, stood on end against the corner of the wagon bed. This one was much heavier. He didn't have to open it to know what was inside.

He wondered whether he should bury the two boxes or bring them along. Leaving them behind was a risk, but carrying them was no less of one. He tried to decide what Liz would want and concluded that it was better to bring them along. If he succeeded in rescuing the women, he didn't want to have to make a detour to recover the boxes. And their contents would buy replacements for everything else in the trunks under the wagon. With plenty left over.

Liz had said it was ten thousand dollars. Even if it was just half that, it was a small fortune.

Now, all he had to do was find the roan. And Barbara. Slocum limped into the trees in the same direction Barbara had gone. He called to her, but got no answer. On his game leg, he found the underbrush tough going. Working his way another ten or fifteen feet into the brush, he stopped and called out again. This time she answered him, but her voice came from some distance away.

"Where are you?" he shouted.

"I'll be right there." Her shout was followed immediately by the rustle of leaves nearly a hundred yards downstream. At that distance, it sounded like paper being rolled into a ball. The sound came steadily closer, punctuated by the snapping of twigs underfoot. A few moments later, Slocum caught a flash of light blue among the leaves.

"What are you doing?" he called.

"I found something we need," she said.

She reached out and brushed away some low-hanging branches, and he could see into the tunnel among the leaves. Barbara had found the horse. She tugged on the reins, and the roan followed her reluctantly, tossing its head every couple of steps.

Slocum started to move toward her, but she stopped him with a raised hand. "Stay there, I can handle it."

A minute later, she stepped out of the brush and pulled the horse impatiently through a clump of trees. "He knows his own mind, doesn't he?" Barbara said, smiling.

"Kind of like his owner," Slocum said. "But he's a special animal. Strong and handsome."

"Kind of like his owner," Barbara mimicked him.

Slocum tipped his hat. "Why, thank you, ma'am. That's mighty nice."

"You sound like a dime novel."

Slocum grinned at her and felt just a little silly. She made him feel like a kid for some reason, and it made him just a bit nervous. He moved a couple of steps closer and took the reins from her hand. He patted the big stallion and looked it over from nose to tail. As far as he could tell, it was none the worse for wear. He checked the boot and was delighted to see that the Winchester was still there.

"Wait here," he said.

"Where are you going?"

"I lost my pistol up in the meadow, there. I want to find it before the grass springs back. Right now, at least I know where to look."

He raised his foot toward the stirrup, wincing as the muscles in his thigh flexed. It felt as if someone had spilled scalding water on him, and he bit his lower lip. Breaking out in a cold sweat, he kept pushing, but the pain was just a little too much for him.

"Why don't you let me go look?" Barbara asked.

"Never mind. I'll have to get up sooner or later. Might as well do it now. First time's the hardest."

"And I suppose you'll just jump right down when you find the pistol and climb right back up? Or do you plan to lean over and grab it with your teeth?"

"Look, Liz is gone. Don't feel you have to fill in for her while she's away."

"I don't think I could," Barbara said, raising an eyebrow sarcastically.

"What's that supposed to mean?"

"Forget it." The smile was gone. She licked her lips with the tip of her tongue, then chewed thoughtfully on the lower one. He thought for a second she was going to tell him anyway, but instead she reached for the reins and jerked them out of his hand before he realized what she was up to.

She was in the saddle before Slocum could say a word and wheeled the roan in a tight circle a second later. She was already on the way up the slope before Slocum recovered from his surprise. He was beginning to think Liz Holcom was not the only one who managed to hide a thing or two about her past. Barbara rode easily, controlling the animal with her wrists and her knees. That she had more than a passing acquaintance with horsemanship was no longer a secret.

Slocum hobbled back to the wagon while Barbara walked the roan in a zigzag pattern, starting at the bottom of the broad swath of crushed grass Slocum's body had carved in the meadow. After about fifteen minutes, she waved. He watched her climb out of the saddle as easily as she had mounted up. She bent over to retrieve something from the grass, then remounted and eased the roan back down the hill.

She stayed in the saddle when she reached Slocum, sitting easily, her arms crossed over the saddle horn. She handed him the pistol. He thanked her, but it was obvious she wanted to say something. "What is it?"

"Why don't you get a more modern weapon?"

"What's wrong with this one?"

"The ammunition is a pain in the neck. A Peacemaker would be a lot easier."

"Newer isn't always better, Barbara."

"Are you sure?" She raised an eyebrow again, and he was beginning to think she was always talking about one more thing than he was.

But he was afraid to ask.

She jumped down and pulled the horse over to the wagon, where she looped the reins around one of the spokes of a rear wheel. "We better get going, don't you think?"

"In a minute," Slocum said. He tucked the two metal boxes into his saddlebags, then laced them shut.

While he worked, Barbara knelt down beside the wagon and opened her trunk again. Without looking inside, she reached under the lid and groped around, leaning in so far her arm was hidden all the way up to her shoulder. When he'd finished with the saddlebags, Slocum stood back and watched, unwilling to ask what she was looking for.

With the cloth of her shirt draw tight by her twisting, he realized her breasts were fuller than he had thought. Her black hair was coiled in a tight bun, and he could see the freckles on the back of her neck, sprinkled almost as liberally as those on her face and chest. Younger than Liz Holcom, she was more muscular as well, as if she had led a rather vigorous life without being ground down by it. She was taller than Liz, too, by three or four inches, all of it leg.

When she found what she was looking for, she turned to

look up at him, and he saw for the first time just how black her eyes were, like pieces of volcanic glass, glittering and impossibly deep at the same time. Where Mabel Shaw was quiet, almost withdrawn, but otherwise nearly a physical replica of Liz Holcom, even to the color of her hair, Barbara McDonough was her antithesis in every conceivable way.

He was trying to remember what Karen looked like, to place her, too, somewhere on the spectrum whose ends seemed to be represented by Liz and the woman in front of him, while he watched her withdraw her arm. When he saw what was in her hand, he backed away involuntarily. The big Colt .45, its barrel gleaming in the sunlight, looked even bigger wrapped in her delicate fist. She handed him the pistol, butt first, and he looked at the intricately etched pearl handle. The two plates were identical, each showing a man in profile, nearly drowning in a full head of curly hair.

"Yours or your husband's?" Slocum asked.

"Mine. But it was my father's, first."

Pointing to the profile carved in the pearl, he said, "Who's this?"

"Johann Sebastian Bach."

"Who?"

"A composer, Johann Bach. My father had three of them done. He gave one to each of my sisters, as well. He said it was to remind us that the gun should be an instrument of civilization, not brutality."

"Wouldn't that be nice!"

"I have bullets, too, in case you're wondering."

"I was, as a matter of fact."

Taking the Colt back, she tucked it in her belt, then fished around in the trunk again, found a box of shells, and set it on the ground. She undid two buttons on her shirt, then pulled the cloth away to reach inside. She watched Slocum watching her, a broad smile on her face. When she brought her hand out, a small key between her fingers, the blue cotton yawned even wider, another button came undone, and he blushed.

She jerked the key over her head, letting the rawhide

cord dangle in the dust while she locked the trunk. "If somebody wants something, I think he ought to work for it a little, don't you?"

Once again he had the unsettling impression her question had nothing to do with the trunk or its contents. He just nodded.

"I guess we better move out," Barbara said. She looped the key back around her neck, tucked in her shirt again, and untied the roan. Slocum couldn't help but notice she hadn't rebuttoned the shirt. While he wondered what that might mean, she vaulted into the saddle. Patting the back of the saddle, she said, "I think you better ride in back." She reached down for his hand, but he didn't respond.

"Well . . . ?" she said.

"I'm alright. I can ride."

"But I can't stay here. That means we both have to ride the same horse. With your leg, I think it best that I take the reins. Besides, you don't want me scratching at your back trying to hang on. It's torn up enough as it is. Isn't it?"

Slocum shook his head. "I guess so. I'll try it, but I don't like it."

Again she reached down, and this time he took her hand, using the right stirrup to swing up on the roan's off side.

"Now hold on tight," she said as he gingerly placed a hand on either of her hips. "No, not like that." Impatiently she tugged his arms forward, then slapped his palms against her ribs. "Somewhere in that general area," she said. "Just don't distract me."

She prodded the roan with her knees before he could answer. A second later, the roan was heading back toward Sterling at a fast trot. "I don't think we can catch them by nightfall," she said.

"I'm more worried about what to do once we *do* catch them."

9

After two hours, the roan was tiring noticeably. Even on the downward side of every hill, his pace seemed sporadic. A missed step here and there signaled the approach of exhaustion. His flanks were flecked with foam, and his breathing was labored. Slocum knew they'd have to rest him soon. If they pushed him too hard for too long, they would burn him out.

"I think we have to take a break soon," he said, leaning over Barbara's shoulder.

"I was just thinking the same thing," she answered. "I think we ought to give him a breather once we bottom out."

Neither of them had said much since leaving the wagon behind. Slocum had spent the time trying to decide what his next step ought to be. It seemed clear that, unless they managed to get a second horse, they had no chance to catch up with McDonald's men before sundown. And once the sun set, he did not want to take the risk of running into them accidentally. To prevent it, they would have to go so slowly, it was pointless to bother. They'd be better off letting the horse recoup his strength and start out fresh in the morning.

"On the way out of Sterling," he asked, "did you pass any place we can get another mount?"

"There was a small ranch about twenty miles out of town. We passed it the second day. They had fifteen or eighteen head in a corral. But I don't know whether any of them were for sale."

"We won't get that far until sometime tomorrow," Slocum said.

"I know, but that was the only place I remember. We can't leave the trail to go looking for a horse. We might never find one and end up wasting all that time."

"One thing looks pretty positive," Slocum said. "I think McDonald won't hurt Liz and the others. If he intended to do that, he wouldn't have bothered to cart them off."

"So, it's Liz now, is it?" Barbara turned to grin at him. He shook his head, and she laughed, sticking her tongue out and making a face.

"You know what I mean," Slocum protested.

"Oh, yes, I do. Better than you think, Mr. Slocum."

"What's that supposed to mean?"

"Just what it says."

Slocum searched desperately for a change of subject. "We have to keep our eyes peeled for an ambush. They're liable to be expecting to be followed."

"I don't think so," she argued. "As far as they know, you're dead and I've run off. At best, I'm stranded out there, and even if I managed to survive, the last thing they'd expect is for me to come chasing after them."

"I'm just telling you what I'd do in their shoes. Better safe than sorry. You have to realize it doesn't cost them anything to have a couple of men hang back, just in case."

"They only had a half dozen or so to begin with."

"How many men does it take to watch three women?"

"Okay, okay, let's say, for the sake of argument, you're right. What can we do about it? We can't detour, not with a single horse for the two of us. We sure can't split up. The only thing we can do is push on."

"But we *can* be careful. That's all I'm suggesting. I don't think we have to change course, just keep our eyes open. If they are planning to bushwhack us, there won't be too many places. You've been over the trail once. Can you remember anyplace that would offer them cover and surprise?"

"No, not really. But there was one place where the trail wound through a deep ravine. If they went up above, they'd have a clear shot without exposing themselves. It was nearly a half mile long. If they let us get well into it, they could take their time and pick their spot. It would be like shooting clay pigeons."

"How good are you with that Peacemaker?"

"As good as I want to be."

"What's that mean? Why are you always talking in riddles?"

"One man's riddle is another man's signpost, Mr. Slocum. Maybe there is less than meets the ear in what I say."

"Yeah, and maybe Abe Lincoln liked the play."

"You're too cynical by half, Mr. Slocum."

He wanted to answer her, but bit his tongue. It seemed like every time he opened his mouth, he stuck his boot in it. He wondered whether she had a point. To admit it would mean he had been reading into things, and to deny it would simply confirm her in her own analysis. A quarter mile later, he was willing to try another tack.

"How far to that ravine?"

"Two, maybe three miles, why?"

They were approaching the bottom of a bowl-shaped depression between two broad, rolling hills. "Let's take a breather and see if we can't figure something out."

Barbara let the horse reach the valley floor, then reined him in. She swung her right leg up and over the horse's head, then jumped to the ground. Slocum envied her the flexibility and wished that the wooden thing hanging from his left side could move so easily.

"You want to get down?" she asked.

Slocum nodded. He started to slide off the horse, but she held up a hand. "Wait a minute," she said.

Turning her back, she moved close to the horse. "Lean over as far as you can. I'll catch you."

"It' alright," Slocum snapped. "I'll manage."

"You open that wound, and it'll cost us even more time. You can't afford to lose any more blood."

She was right, and Slocum did as he was told, wrapping his legs around her waist. Barbara leaned forward, took two steps, and waited for him to lower his right leg. When he felt it could take his weight, he let the left leg go, then unwrapped his arms from around her neck.

"You're stronger than you look," Slocum said.

"It's in the eye of the beholder," she said. "You see a woman, and all you can think about is petticoats and cooking. That wasn't my life. Not now, and not ever."

"What *was* your life?"

"If we get out of this, maybe I'll tell you," she said.

"I'd like that."

"I bet you won't . . ."

She let the horse wander off into the grass. He seemed almost too tired to graze. Tugging listlessly at the taller blades, the horse chewed noisily for a while, drifting closer to a small spring full of reeds. When he got close enough, he lowered his head and lapped at the water, more like a puppy than a full-grown stallion.

"I suppose you want to know about the ravine . . ." Barbara knelt, not waiting for his answer. She ripped several handfuls of grass out by the roots, exposing a patch of dry ground. With one slender finger, she sketched a pair of squiggly lines in the dirt. "It's about a half mile or so long. The west wall is about fifty feet high, the east wall another ten feet or so."

"I guess we can expect them on the east wall, then. Is there a back way, some way we can get up behind them?"

"I don't know. We came through the bottom. With the wagon, it was the only way."

"We can try the east wall or we can try the west," Slocum said, thinking aloud rather than suggesting an approach. "The ten feet gives them the advantage, but they probably won't be expecting us to go that way."

"We could try both," Barbara suggested. "You can take the horse one way, and I can go the other on foot. It'll cost us a little time, but I'll bet not much. It's so rocky, I can probably move almost as fast as you could on the horse."

"And suppose you run into them?"

She patted the butt of the Peacemaker sticking out of her dungarees. "What do you think this is for?"

"I can't let you do that. It's too dangerous." And he knew, as soon as he said it, that there was no way he could talk her out of it. He sighed. "Alright, alright."

"I'm a big girl, Slocum. I can take care of myself."

"We could wait until nightfall. They probably won't expect us to try it in the dark."

"Why waste the time? We're not even sure anybody's waiting for us. I think we should get on with it. If we catch up with them before they get to Sterling, we'll have a better chance to rescue them."

"I suppose."

"Why are you doing this, anyway? You don't owe us anything."

"A deal's a deal, Miss McDonough."

"This wasn't part of any deal, Slocum, was it? And it's Barbara."

"I said I'd help. And I aim to do just that. Besides, I'm not in the habit of walking away from somebody who tried to kill me."

"You can carry that southern gentleman routine too far, you know. You can make a fool of yourself for some distorted sense of honor. If that's what's behind it, it's not too late to change your mind."

"What would you do if I did?"

"I don't know."

"Would you walk away from it?"

"Probably not."

"Well, then, I guess that settles it. Two fools are better than one."

Barbara stood up and walked over to the horse. She stood near his head, still bent to lap water and tug a few blades of grass every now and then. She grabbed the reins and pulled the roan away from the spring. "Come on, big fellow," she said. "It's time to go. You too, Slocum," she said, smiling over her shoulder.

She led the horse back to Slocum and swung into the saddle. Like the first time, she helped him up. This time, he felt strangely at ease, as if already they had a routine both were comfortable with.

When he was ensconced on the rear lip of the saddle, she asked, "How's your leg?"

"Some better," he said. "Still stiff, but it doesn't hurt as much as it did."

"We'll have to get it looked at as soon as we can."

"First things first."

She didn't answer, instead clucking to the horse and squeezing him with her knees. He moved off at a walk. "I think we better save his strength. He'll need it for the climb."

Slocum just grunted.

A half hour later, they sat on a low ridge looking down to where the trail wound into the mouth of a ravine. "That's it," she said. The eastern edge of the ravine was nearly as high as the ridge on which they sat. But they had a mile downhill before they could begin their climbs up the opposing sides. Slocum used his binoculars to check both sides. The angle was too flat to let him see all the way to the other end, but he saw no evidence they were expected.

"Looks deserted," he said.

"If you were up there, you'd be someplace in the middle, wouldn't you?"

"Yup."

"They probably are too. My dad used to say the worse mistake you can make is thinking you're smarter than the other guy."

"Your dad was a smart man."

"Smartest man I ever met."

"Let's do it, then," Slocum said, squeezing her ribs to get her moving.

"I might get used to that," she said, nudging the horse down the front side of the ridge.

"Don't," Slocum said.

"That part of the deal too?"

"Yup."

"You agree to that before Liz climbed into the saddle, or after?"

Slocum inhaled sharply. But he said nothing. Barbara let it go. Neither of them spoke on the slow descent. Barbara angled the horse away from the mouth of the ravine, trying to buy as much cover as she could. It would make her walk longer, but she thought it was a small enough price to pay.

On the valley floor, she jumped down from the saddle, and Slocum slid forward. His left leg throbbed when he bent it far enough to slip his foot into the stirrup. Barbara watched him closely, but said nothing, even when he bit down on his lower lip.

"All set?" Slocum asked.

Instead of responding, Barbara unbuckled a saddlebag and took out the box of .45 shells. She opened it and tilted half the shells into her hand, stuffing them into the pockets of her dungarees. "If I need any more than that, I probably don't have enough anyway," she smiled. She shoved the box back into the saddlebag and rebuckled it.

Then she was on her way through the underbrush, and he lost sight of her for several minutes. He was just starting to worry when he caught a glimpse of light blue in the brush across the mouth of the canyon. She started her climb, and Slocum nudged his horse to the right. The ascent was steep, and the brush heavy enough to whip his legs unmercifully.

Halfway up, he spotted a pile of fresh horse dung, and he knew they had been right to worry. Whether they had worried enough, he would soon find out.

10

Near the top of the broad hill, Slocum was getting nervous. The horse was making more noise than he could afford. Between the tangled brush and the stony ground, there was no way to keep his passage quiet. Since the bushwhackers, if they were there at all, could be anywhere along the rim of the ravine, he had to find some way to negotiate it quietly.

Despite the pain in his leg, Slocum slid off the horse, using a boulder as a step and letting his right leg take all of his weight. Once on the ground, he tried walking, but it was not easy going. He could manage it if he didn't have to move too quickly, but it was all but impossible for him to keep a low profile. Any flexing at all of the left leg sent a white-hot sword stabbing through the torn thigh muscle.

He had to find some way to control the pain, to give himself much needed mobility. He took one of the loose saddlebag straps and cut the flap off the bag itself. Wrapping it around his leg, he cinched the thigh with the belt and pulled it tight, to see how far down the strap he needed to punch a new hole. When he had the strap drawn as tightly as he could, he gouged a new hole for the buckle tine to go through and buckled it above the wound. Taking the strap from the other saddlebag, he measured it and cut a new hole in it as well. When the second strap was tight, this one below the wound, he tried flexing his leg.

It still hurt, but he could move more freely now, and the pain was manageable. Slocum took the Winchester from its boot and extra shells from the open saddlebag. Tethering the horse to a scrub pine, Slocum started off through the boulders, keeping to a crouch as much as possible. The lip of the ravine was heavily strewn with boulders, and the rest of the ground was littered with smaller rocks. They cracked and ground together under his boots, but the noise was not nearly as loud as it had been under the horse's hooves.

Picking his way carefully through the gaps and niches among the huge rocks, he zigzagged along the rim, stopping every twenty yards or so to listen. He watched the far rim, about fifty yards away, for signs of Barbara, but he hadn't seen a trace of her since that one flash of light blue as she began her ascent.

The leg ached, but it was a dull throb instead of the sharp, stabbing pain he'd felt before. He used the Winchester as a cane over the rougher spots and bent the left leg as little as possible, swinging it forward in a stiff-legged strut whenever he could. Back away from the edge of the canyon, he couldn't see its floor, and he had no idea how long the ravine was. In a way, he was just as glad. Not knowing made it less intimidating.

Thunder rolled down off the mountains behind him, and Slocum turned to see a huge thunderhead towering high overhead. As he watched, it flattened out and seemed to slide downhill. It blotted out the sun for a long minute, while repeated peals of thunder made the ground shake. A spear of jagged lightning bleached the sky and left its image in his eyes for a few seconds, then it darkened all over as a heavy mass of clouds slid in behind the thunderhead.

Slocum moved faster now, knowing the weather would cover incidental noise. As the wind picked up, shaking the scrub pine and gnarled sumac clinging to the rocky rim, he felt a chill. Sheet lightning flashed intermittently, throwing his shadow on the rocks in front of him. The first drop of rain hit him in the back like a shotgun pellet. Another and a third slammed into him, leaving silver dollar-sized spots on Barbara's shirt, then harder rain started to rattle all around him. It took him a moment to realize it wasn't rain at all, but hail, the stones bigger than minnie balls, clattering on the rocks and shattering into slivers of flying ice.

The footing was getting treacherous. The hailstones seemed to accumulate in bunches, rolling into hollows in the earth and clinging together. He avoided them when he could and stepped gingerly when he couldn't. He ignored the added strain on his injured leg and pushed on, driving himself to the limit. He nearly slipped on another pile of fresh horse droppings and cursed softly as he wiped off the sole of his boot.

He had still seen no sign of anyone else on the rim, but there was no point in turning back now. Slipping in between two boulders, he ducked involuntarily as a lightning bolt slammed into a solitary pine fifty yards ahead. The tree seemed to split lengthwise and exploded as its sap boiled and tore the tree to pieces. The thunder was so loud it took him a moment before he realized what it was. His ears were ringing, and the brilliant slash of lightning was seared into his vision.

Slocum closed his eyes and crouched down behind a tall, flattened rock. He shook his head to try to get rid of the bells still tolling inside it and rubbed his eyes with his palms. The hail kept banging into him like spent shot, and he could feel the welts on his back starting to tingle where they'd been hit. His hat protected his head from the hailstones except for a narrow ribbon just above the brim, where his skull was flush up against the Stetson. But there was no place to take cover, and he wanted to take advantage of the unexpected diversion offered by the storm.

Darting, as best he could, from boulder to boulder, Slocum stopped using the Winchester as a crutch. It slowed him down too much, and he'd rather endure the added pain in favor of ready firepower. He snicked the safety off and levered a shell into the carbine's chamber, then hobbled another fifteen yards. He felt almost foolish in his contorted strut.

He looked across the ravine to the edge of the lower wall. It was farther away at this point, and he could barely see it as fog swirled through the hills, gray rags whipped into a frenzy by the gusting wind. Gray seemed to boil up out of the ravine like thick smoke, as if the mouth of hell were down there below him. The hair stood up on the back of his neck, and he had the distinct sensation that if he were to slip over the edge, he would be swallowed whole before he ever hit the ground.

Another thunder clap rolled up behind him, and in its aftermath, he heard the faint, but distinct, whinny of a frightened horse. He stopped to listen, but the sound was not repeated. Somewhere ahead, a horse and, presumably, its rider waited. There could be no doubt it waited for him and for Barbara. There could be no other reason for anyone to secrete himself among the rocks up here.

Slocum moved again, more carefully. The hail was beginning to slacken, changing to a steady downpour. The dirt underfoot began to thicken, clinging to his boots in thick clots and making his progress more difficult. In spots, it was slippery, the bare rock just a couple of inches down covered with a slimy paste. He lost his footing once and slammed into a rock with his left knee. The shock seemed to radiate out through every bone in his body, ricochet back along the skeleton, and come to rest in one huge, throbbing knot in his left thigh.

He heard the horse again, much closer, and he stopped to peer through the swirling mist. The tattered fog darted in and out among the rocks like ghosts among tombstones. Things hidden for a moment jumped out at him while others vanished as if they had dissolved before his eyes.

If there was a man ahead, Slocum knew he could trip over him without even realizing he was there. But he had no choice. He moved to the right, skirting away from the rimrock and hoping he could slide in behind the horse and, if all went according to plan, its rider.

Another nicker, and hooves clopped on the rocks. The animal couldn't be more than fifty or sixty feet away now. Slocum stopped again, trying to see through the spiraling wisps of fog. The rain came down even harder, slashing sheets slicing across his field of vision like bands of shimmering silver foil. And a hat, almost hidden behind a cluster of tall rocks, moved up and turned to the left. Black, it looked more like a shadow than not, but Slocum was sure even before it dropped out of sight.

He waited to see if the man moved again, holding his breath as long as he could, then letting it out in a thin stream between clenched teeth. He could see the horse in the glare from another flash of lightning, its mane a drape of thin ropes trailing thin silver streams. The animal was plainly skittish, and it danced nervously in place, tossing its head as the lightning pulsed for several moments, one great flare followed by a dozen flickers before it went out altogether.

Shifting his position, Slocum eased closer. The horse was sensitized and might give him away if the rider was paying any attention at all to his mount. The black hat appeared again and below it a pair of broad shoulders in a rain-darkened canvas slicker. Slocum had a clear shot, but he was no backshooter. He'd have to get closer or risk a Mexican standoff. Once the man knew he was there, they could trade shots until hell froze over. There was just too much cover for both of them. Neither man had any advantage but surprise. For the hidden gunman, it was already gone. Slocum still had it, but he could feel it slipping off the tips of his fingers, washed away as easily as dust by the torrential rain.

Twenty feet away, and he still couldn't cover the cowboy completely. He'd have to climb in among the same cluster of boulders to make sure. And Barbara was on the opposite rim, possibly creeping up behind another man. If Slocum lost his edge, hers might go with it.

Ten feet away, and still he had to get closer. In midstride, he almost lost his balance. The Winchester slipped out of his hands just as another peal of thunder started, far off, like a huge piece of cloth beginning to rip. It sounded as if the sky were made of canvas and God had decided to tear it up and throw it away. It ended in the loudest explosion Slocum had ever heard.

He bent to retrieve the rifle, hoping the man had heard nothing under the thunder. His hand found the stock, his fingers closed over the mud-slick walnut and he was starting to lift it when he heard the shot. It was distant, almost not a sound at all. He thought he might have imagined it when the man in the black hat stood straight up and cupped his hands to shout into the wind, "Clay? You alright? Clay? You hear me?"

The wind ripped the words away, and Slocum was certain they didn't travel fifty feet before degenerating into unintelligible muttering. The black hat seemed to decide the same thing, and he moved toward the horse. He had a carbine in his hands and held it high, ready to slip it into the boot, when Slocum lost his grip a second time.

The Winchester slammed into hard stone with a crack. In one of those peculiar silences that seem to come out of nowhere in the heart of a whirlwind, for a second it was the only noise. The cowboy heard it and stopped, his carbine frozen for an instant before he turned.

Slocum reached for the Winchester again and lost his balance. He landed hard on his shoulder and pinned the gun under him. Desperately, he grabbed the Colt on his hip, bringing it up as the cowboy jerked the lever on his carbine. The man's mouth opened, but a thunder clap drowned out whatever he'd tried to say. It looked as if he had uttered the thunder himself as Slocum pulled the trigger once, then again.

The Colt jerked in his hand, and he fired a third time. The cowboy reached for his shoulder as the carbine disappeared. He staggered back a step, letting go of the reins.

Then he disappeared. Slocum heard the scream echo up from the ravine for a moment. Then he heard only the wind and the sound of rain beating on his hat.

Rushing to the edge of the ravine, Slocum looked down into the blackness. In another flash of lightning, he saw the rocks and a band of silver where runoff coursed through the canyon bottom. He turned back and retrieved the cowboy's carbine. Grabbing his own rifle, he booted the carbine, untethered the frightened horse, and coached it back through the jumbled rocks. Standing on a boulder, he climbed into the saddle and urged the horse back the way he'd come. It was no longer necessary to keep silent. But the going was treacherous.

The horse picked his way carefully, resisting Slocum's effort to make him go faster. The rain began to let up, but it was still dark, and the fog continued to whirl in the wind in scraps and pieces. When he reached the roan, Slocum untethered him and hooked the reins on his saddle. Leading the stallion downhill, he found himself listening intently, but still there was no further noise from the far rim of the ravine.

He tied the roan to a tree and started up the far side, kicking the horse now, as the rain died to a drizzle. The clouds overhead scudded on a brisk wind, and gaps of light appeared and disappeared here and there. At the top of the ravine, he found evidence that at least one horse had recently passed that way as well. His leg had begun to throb again, and he could feel it stiffening up. He thought he might have torn the wound open again, but there was no way to tell whether the dampness in his boot was blood or rainwater.

Slocum didn't know whether to be encouraged or frightened by the silence. The gunshots he'd heard had been almost obscured by the howling wind.

Ten minutes later, he found her. She was motionless, her head to one side, her back against a granite slab. Slocum leapt from the horse and hobbled toward her, oblivious of the pain in his thigh.

The body next to her lay on its back, a dark red blur covering the man's shirt front. Barbara's pistol lay on the ground between the two motionless forms. Slocum knelt beside her. "Barbara?" he said. She didn't answer, and he shook her so hard her head bounced off the rock behind her. "Barbara?"

"I never killed anyone before," she whispered. "I hate the way I feel."

11

The sun came out as they started downhill. Brilliant spears of light radiated out from behind banks of clouds, banding the sky with white against the purple and blue-black remnants of the storm. Barbara rode the captured horse, following in Slocum's wake. She hadn't said more than a dozen words since Slocum found her. The cockiness was gone. Even her body seemed somehow different, as if it had collapsed in around her, the flesh desperately hugging the bones.

They could make better time now, but Slocum was worried. His volatile ally had suddenly become a dead weight. It was almost as if it had been a lark for her, until she had pulled the trigger. Slocum had seen that reaction before. During the war, some new recruit, a dead shot who could put a ball through a washer at a hundred yards, shoot the eyes out of a hawk on the wing, suddenly came face-to-face with consequences. Seeing your first victim, dead eyes looking up at an empty sky, the limbs carelessly splayed, the stench beginning to attract bugs, that was something that had nothing to do with competence.

That was death in its purest and most concentrated form. The recognition of that fact was a one-time thing. And with it came the knowledge that one day the splayed limbs could be yours, the bugs could be crawling in your own ears. And there is no way in hell, Slocum thought, you can sugarcoat that kind of understanding. It changes you forever.

Glancing back at Barbara's slumped shoulders, the stony set of her face, the white knuckles squeezing the reins in a mindless contraction, he realized that she had learned something about herself that she would never forget, and that she might never be able to forgive, either. He wanted to console her, but he had nothing to say. Words were pointless at a time like this. They bounced off an invisible screen, glancing away harmlessly, like peas from a peashooter hitting a stone wall.

Barbara was a new, and different, person. That was the central fact of what had happened. She didn't need him to tell her about it. And it wasn't possible to pretend that the new knowledge would ever be less painful to confront.

The clouds seemed to evaporate as they rode on, but the sun was evaporating too, sliding down the far side of the Rockies and disappearing. It cast long red-tinged shadows ahead of them, figures that mocked them, making every move they made, like spiteful children mimicking parents.

They had a decision to make, and Slocum didn't want to make it on his own. They were still thirty miles from Sterling. But he didn't want to waste time. They could push the horses, but progress in the dark would be painfully slow. If they spent the night on the trail, they could start out at sunup, maybe close the gap a little. But it was too soon to pose the question. Barbara was still numb. He wouldn't be surprised if she didn't want to continue the pursuit at all. And he wouldn't blame her if she didn't.

The last bit of red sun vanished and they had at best twenty minutes of daylight left. Already the valley was full of shadows. The trail was rough, and it wouldn't take much to lose it altogether in the darkness. They settled into the valley bottom, and Slocum pulled back on the reins, nudging his horse to one side. He waited for Barbara to come abreast of him. She reined in her own mount.

She looked at him with an expressionless face. Dull, flat eyes stared at him, but they seemed to see nothing.

"Why are you stopping?" she asked.

"I don't think we can go any farther tonight."

"Why not?"

"It's too dark. The horses are spent." He patted her arm. "And you've been through a lot. You're exhausted."

"I'm alright."

"No, you're not alright. You don't even know how far

from alright you are. But I know. I've been there."

"What difference does it make? I can't change anything."

"No, maybe not. But a little rest will make things better."

"Why? Will that man be alive in the morning?"

Slocum didn't answer right away. When he did, he realized he couldn't lie to her. He couldn't tell her that anything would be different. He knew it wasn't true. And he knew that she knew it, too. If he tried to lie to her, she would stop trusting him, and the fragile thread of trust was already beginning to fray. "No, of course not. You know better than that."

"Then what difference does it make?"

"You need time to accept it, that's all. You can't do that when you're exhausted."

"How many men have you killed, Mr. Slocum?"

"I don't know." He was taken aback by the question. His horse sensed his nervousness and shifted beneath him, tossing its head and tugging at the reins. "A few."

"Is it always like this?"

"You mean, does it ever feel better?"

"No, I mean does it feel different the second time?"

"No, it doesn't."

"Then why did you do it again?"

"Things happen," Slocum said. His explanation sounded feeble in his own ears, but he pushed on with it. "Sometimes you don't have any choice. Some people will push and push until you push back. Sometimes, they back down. And sometimes they don't."

"So you kill them . . ."

"No. I mean, not me personally. People. It's the way people are. Somebody is always willing to take what isn't his, to use people in ways they don't want to be used. The choice you have, sometimes, is being made to do something you don't want to do, or letting someone take something of yours . . . or feeling like this. But if you let the feeling stop you, they win. It's what they count on. They *know* they can kill you. They think you won't kill them, or can't. There's really no difference. I don't know where you're from, Miss McDonough, but wherever it is, I guarantee you it's different."

"People are people, Mr. Slocum."

He thought about that for a minute before answering. "Yeah, that's true," he said. "The trouble is, some people are animals. You can't reason with a wild animal. And you can't reason with some people. That man was there for one reason, to stop you and me. He would have done anything he had to. That's why he was there. And chances are, it was just a job for him. He was on somebody's payroll, and that somebody told him to do whatever it took."

"But I showed him, didn't I?" Her voice was still almost inflectionless, but the bitter irony was there in her eyes, in the way her mouth curved at the corners. There was no pride in the statement, and no joy. Just a sad recognition that Slocum was telling her the truth, and the truth was unpleasant.

"Look, he would have killed you. You didn't let him. You can feel bad about what you had to do. But you don't have to blame yourself. That's what'll be better in the morning. When you can think more clearly, you'll see that. You'll understand that he's dead and you're not, but through no fault of yours."

"And I'll learn to accept that, will I?"

"Yes."

"No, Mr. Slocum, I won't. I will try to learn to admit it to myself, but I'll never learn to accept it. I can't, not something like that."

"You can do a lot more than you think."

"No. Never..."

She turned away, and her shoulders shook. Slocum dismounted and stepped close to her horse. He reached up to her. At first, she didn't react. Then, when she could contain herself no longer, she nearly fell from the horse. With her head buried in his shoulder, she began to sob. Her whole body trembled, and Slocum held her close. It was too late to prevent what had happened. She knew that now. Time had already begun its healing.

But it would be a long process. And Slocum didn't have the heart to tell her it never ended.

"I'm alright," she blubbered. "I'm alright now."

It was a brave lie, and Slocum went along. "I guess I'll get some wood for a fire," he said.

It was easier said than done. The torrential downpour had soaked everything in sight. Slocum rooted around under brush and small scrub pines, looking for enough dry branches to get something going. Once he got a small fire, there was plenty of wood he could dry before throwing it on the blaze. It took fifteen minutes to get enough tinder, and it resisted the match at first. When he finally got a small flame, he cupped his hands around it as if it were the last one on earth.

Barbara appeared behind him, a stack of small branches in her arms, and dropped them to the ground. Slocum urged the flame on, got it to spread a bit, and soon had a steady, crackling fire going. He arranged the branches close enough to dry them, fed the fire slowly, and let it build without choking it.

Barbara came back with more wood, larger pieces now, and together they arranged them within the circle of heat. "That ought to hold us," Slocum said. They had selected a small crevice among a pile of boulders, enough to give them cover on all sides. They could do nothing to conceal the smoke or the flames themselves, but at least they'd be protected from a long-range shot.

The crevice was large enough for them to spread bedrolls, but not much more. For their meal, they contented themselves with dried meat and a cup of rainwater. Too tired to realize how hungry they were, they huddled close to the flames, letting its heat soak into their bones. Their clothes dried on their bodies, the cloth stiff and sticking to their skins.

Barbara sat with her back against a rock, her knees drawn up and her chin resting in the crevice between them. The flames changed the color of her eyes, the crystalline black suddenly full of fire. Her hair, too, picked up highlights from the flames. Her freckles seemed to glow with reflected light. She was so motionless she might have been a statue.

Slocum closed his eyes, curling up in his blanket. It had been soaked by the rain, and it steamed now where the heat hit it. "If you want to talk, tell me," he said.

She didn't answer, but he heard her move. When her hand touched his shoulder, he opened his eyes. She was kneeling beside him. "I don't want to talk," she said. "I just don't want to be alone."

Slocum slid over and made room for her close to the fire. She lay on her stomach and he pulled the blanket over her. He draped an arm across her shoulders. Barbara had her chin on her folded hands. He watched her quietly. Her eyes staring off into the darkness, she seemed to be thinking about nothing at all, as if her mind were asleep. When she blinked, the night was so quiet he thought he could hear the whisper of her lashes.

"Tell me about your husband," he said.

She shook her head. "Tell me about Liz," she said.

"There's nothing to tell."

"I know what I saw. You seemed to be enjoying yourself. Were you?"

"What you saw?"

"Last night, up on the hillside."

"You *saw* us? What the hell were you doing up there?"

"Don't be angry."

"Why were you spying on us?"

"I wasn't spying. I just . . ."

"What?"

"Never mind."

She didn't answer him for a long time. She closed her eyes, and he thought she might have fallen asleep. She shook her head after a minute. "I just . . . I guess I wanted . . ."

"Spit it out."

"I went up there to do what she did, alright? Are you satisfied?"

"To do what she did? What are you talking about?"

"If you don't know, I guess I didn't miss anything. Huh, Slocum?" She turned to him. Tears had pooled in her eyes, but she was smiling. "Did I, Slocum, did I miss anything?"

Slocum turned away.

"I don't know."

"I guess I'll have to ask Liz, then, won't I."

"Do whatever you want."

"I can't. Liz already did it for you."

"No, as a matter of fact, Liz did it for *you*."

Barbara laughed. "For *me*? How very sweet . . . Did I enjoy it?"

"I don't think so."

"Did you?"

Now it was Slocum's turn to be silent.

12

Sterling was thriving. What had started out as a fur exchange sixty years before, and then become a military outpost, had exploded with the arrival of the cattle barons and the discovery of silver in Colorado. It couldn't offer an opera house, like Denver, and it was anything but civilized, but it was prosperous. Every month at least one wagonload of easterners who found the trek overland to the Pacific Northwest more than they bargained for decided that Sterling was as far west as they had the strength to go. It was home to more than three thousand people, and the nearest thing to a city for several thousand more.

On the last ridge outside of town, Slocum sat restlessly in the saddle. They had come all the way back without seeing a single trace of McDonald or his captives. He was beginning to wonder whether they had made the wrong choice, if perhaps McDonald had outsmarted them after all. The only proof he hadn't was the ambush. And that had to be McDonald's doing. Not only because Slocum didn't want to be wrong, but because he knew Barbara would go to pieces if she believed she had killed a man for no reason at all.

The town sported three hotels, and the only logical thing for them to do was to take a room at one of them and start looking. The quicker they moved, the better chance they had to find Liz and the others. Barbara insisted they should take a room together. All she had to do was to tuck her hair up under her hat and make sure her shirt fit her badly. Her point was well taken. With space at a premium, most hotels crammed strangers together, whether they liked it or not. Beds were to be slept in. Since they'd have to share anyway, she argued, it might as well be with one another.

She had seemed a little better in the morning. Now, with another full day under her belt, she was almost back to normal. He still caught her staring off into space once in a while, and she didn't laugh as easily. But she was tough and resilient. If he could get her to hang together for another couple of days, she'd be okay.

And she had better be. McDonald held just about all the cards. For the moment, he didn't know they were there. But that wouldn't last long. In a day or two, when his hired guns didn't show, he'd start to wonder. A day or two after that, he'd be sure.

Slocum dismounted, and Barbara followed suit. "We have got to change your looks a little," he said.

"I was already thinking about that. Maybe I can just put my hair up. Maybe that'll do it." Slocum looked skeptical.

"It's someplace to start," she said.

Barbara twisted her hair into a tight bun, mounting it high on her head with a pair of tortoise-shell combs. The hat hid the hair easily, but it couldn't do much to conceal the perfection of her skin. Slocum handled that with a handful of dust and grit from the trail. Then he spit on a finger and made a muddy smear down one cheek.

"I don't know," he said. "Maybe it's because I know you, but you still look like a woman to me."

"That's very comforting."

Her breasts were not so easily disguised. She tore some cloth off a spare shirt and turned away from him to open her shirt. She bound her breasts as flat as she could, then buttoned the shirt back up.

Slocum shook his head, laughing. "Nope. There's just a little too much of you there not to look like you."

"Well I don't know what else to do," she snapped.

"Maybe stuff a little something in there, plump up a bit, or something." Mumbling to herself she turned away and stuffed the rest of the ruined shirt in, then turned back.

"Nice gut you got there." Slocum grinned.

"Maybe we should forget it. You can sneak me inside later."

"My roommate might take exception to that. No, this is

the only way to go. I just hope we can pull it off."

"What about my hips?"

"Very nice. Not too big, but plenty solid. I like them. Turn around."

She stamped a foot, but did as he told her. He smacked her ass with an open palm. "*This* will attract some attention. Maybe you best wear a duster. If you keep your head down, I guess your toes won't give us away." He jerked a smelly duster from his saddlebag and tossed it to her. "Just roll the sleeves up, if they're too long."

He climbed back into the saddle and clucked to the roan. They rode the long, sweeping approach in silence. They heard the bustle of the town when they were only halfway down. It was nearly sunset, and the saloons would start to get raucous. An hour after that, a gunfight would be narrowly averted, and three or four chairs broken over shoulders. It would be a typical night in a typical western town. Except for one thing: Somewhere in this town, three women who didn't want to be there at all would be wondering how, or if, they'd ever get away.

Slocum was already wondering. It looked like an uphill battle all the way. Finding them would only be the first, and maybe the easiest, step. Getting them out alive would be far less easy.

Entering the town, Slocum noticed how well kept the main street was. He mentioned it to Barbara, who shrugged. Unlike most cattle towns and mining towns, the street was free of ruts, as if someone periodically took care of evening it out. It had to take heavy traffic, not only from horses, but from wagons and stages. The heavy iron wheels raised hell with the packed dirt every time it rained. Most towns didn't worry about the ruts, figuring, if they noticed at all, that the same thing would happen the next time it rained.

"What do you know about McDonald?" Slocum asked as they let their horses walk through the center of the main street.

"Not much. I know he has a lot of influence here, but I don't know why. His money, I guess."

"He can't have that much, just from running a whore-house."

"It's a good business, I understand."

"I wouldn't know."

"Customers seldom know much about the people they buy from, I suppose."

"That was uncalled for."

"I'm sorry, if it was."

"But you don't think so."

"Did you pay Liz?"

"*No*, I didn't pay her."

"Then I'm sorry." Barbara's lips were a white line behind the smeared trail dirt. Then, as if a sudden thought occurred to her, she said, "Did she pay *you*?"

"Barbara, what the hell's wrong with you? Of course she didn't pay me. Look, you better pull yourself together. McDonald had two men out there who would have killed us both, as like as not. If I get killed, I want it to be because I deserve it, not because my partner didn't pay attention to her job."

"So, we're partners, now, are we?"

"Not for long, if you keep this up."

"I'll be good. I just . . . oh, never mind!"

"Tell me everything you know about McDonald."

"Not here. Wait until we get a room. I just . . . I feel nervous, or something. Maybe it's crazy, but I just don't think it's a good idea to talk about him in public. Not here, anyway."

"Alright." Slocum sighed.

The Paradise Hotel was the first one they came to. Slocum looked at Barbara, but didn't have to ask.

"Might as well," she said.

Slocum dismounted. "Look, I'll go in, see if they have a room for two. If I don't come out in a few minutes, then you go on and take the horses to the livery stable. I'll sign us in and meet you in the lobby."

She didn't answer right away. Slocum waited a few seconds, then said, "Is that alright?"

Barbara nodded, still without saying anything.

"Are you okay?" he asked. Again she just shook her

head. Puzzled, Slocum turned to enter the hotel. The double glass doors were open to catch what little breeze there was. The lobby was decorated with that exuberant bad taste that marked so much of western decor. It seemed as if someone had brought west parodic sketches of the lavish eastern hotels and spread them around. Too much brocade, too much thick, oppressively dark draperies, just plain too much of everything, as if the great size of the plains demanded tons where ounces would have served.

He crossed to the bell desk and asked a nervous little man in sleeve garters and a bow tie if a room for two was available.

The man nodded and turned the ledger around for Slocum to sign in. "Just two of us," Slocum said again. "I don't want to share with somebody I don't know."

The clerk shook his head. "Sir, this is not a roadhouse. It is a respectable hotel, a civilized establishment. Naturally, you won't be asked to share your privacy with a stranger."

"Just making sure," Slocum said. "You know, some hotels . . ."

"Those are not hotels," the clerk interrupted. "The Paradise is a hotel, those are just bunkhouses."

"Whatever you say." Slocum smiled. He scribbled his name, then asked the clerk to wait a minute. At the front door, he waved to Barbara, watched her move off with the roan in tow, then went back to the desk.

"Will you be staying long?" the clerk asked.

"I'm not sure. I guess I better plan on a week, though, if that's possible."

The clerk nodded. "Ten dollars. In advance."

"Kind of steep, isn't it?" Slocum asked.

"Privacy is a scarce commodity, Mr."—he paused to look at the ledger, still facing away from him—"Slocum."

Slocum took a ten-dollar gold piece out of his pocket and clapped it on the polished wood. "I guess so," he sighed.

The clerk took the coin and handed him a thick key. "Room twenty-one. Up the stairs and to the left. It'll be on your right-hand side. Any luggage?"

Slocum shook his head. "Nope. I'll just wait here for my partner, before I go on up, though. Thank you."

"If you need anything, just let someone at the desk know."

Slocum walked across the lobby, his boots clomping on the clean wooden floor. Long, heavily padded sofas were arranged at right angles in one corner. He sat on the end of the sofa nearest the door.

A striking redhead swept down the semicircular stairs, her elaborate gown clinging to her shoulders. He watched in amusement, wondering if the dress would reach the lobby before she did. It appeared to be touch and go for a minute, but the race ended in a tie. A moment later, a tall, thin man, wearing English tweed and a monocle, descended the stairs after her. She greeted him at the bottom. The couple walked out of the hotel and Slocum wondered where such elegance wouldn't be out of place in a town like Sterling.

Barbara came in a moment later, saddlebags draped over her shoulder, the duster nearly dragging the floor. In one hand she carried a battered carpetbag. Slocum stood up quickly and joined her at the door. He grinned at her. "I'd take these bags, but it might look strange."

She nodded. "Of course."

He led the way to the staircase and started up. He didn't turn around until he was in the hallway above. She looked at him impassively. "Where's the room?" She tried to deepen her voice, but it didn't work. He laughed and she kicked at him, narrowly missing the shin of his bad leg.

Still chuckling, he moved down the hall, checking the doors until he found number twenty-one, identified by bright brass numerals nailed to the doorframe above it. He opened the door and stepped inside. Moving out of the way, he waited until the door was closed before pointing to the one large bed.

"It seems there are limits even at the Paradise." He smiled.

"The floor won't hurt you," she said.

"Not if I don't sleep on it."

"Oh, but you will."

"Don't you trust me?"

"Should I trust a man like you, Slocum?"

He placed a hand over his heart. "I am an honorable man, you have my word."

"You forget, I saw you thrashing around in the weeds under that tart."

"Those are rather harsh words for the woman who just wanted to save you from a fate worse than death."

"And she has, Mr. Slocum. She has. All I want to do is return the favor."

She dropped the saddlebags onto a small table. The metal boxes in the one good bag clunked against the wood. "I want a bath," she said. Then, glancing at Slocum with a brilliant smile, she said, "But don't get any ideas."

"I wouldn't think of it."

She didn't look as if she believed him.

13

Slocum changed clothes quickly, using the bathroom for privacy. He noticed an elaborate tub with cold and hot water taps, but a neat little sign informed him that hot water had to be brought in by the hotel staff. He was in too much of a hurry to worry about such luxury and contented himself with a quick splash of the cold and some soap that smelled far too much of flowers and not enough of good old-fashioned lye.

He was ready in ten minutes, and Barbara sat on the bed watching him. "Where are you going?" she asked.

"To see if I can get a lead on McDonald. Why?"

"Be careful."

"Don't worry."

"Do you have any idea where to start?"

"No. But I imagine a drink or two in a saloon will get me all the information I need."

"Don't bother. Try the French Quarter. It's McDonald's ... establishment. That's where he took us. That's where we met Liz. It's got to be as good a place as any to start."

"Where is it?"

"Up the street, on the left. You can't miss it. It's probably the loudest place in town. They have a piano player and somebody is usually making a fool of himself singing along."

"Thanks."

"Don't mention it. And whatever you do, don't tell me what happened, when you get back."

"It's that bad, huh?"

"Worse."

Slocum nodded. "Look, I think you better stay here

while I'm out. McDonald's people don't know me from Adam, but they might recognize you, even in that get-up."

"I really would like a bath," she said.

"I'll have them send up the hot water. I'll hang around until it's delivered. Then I want you to lock the door and stay in. Understand?"

"Yes."

Slocum opened the door, taking the key with him, then walked down to the lobby. The officious little man behind the desk was still there, shuffling papers and fiddling nervously with his sleeve garters. Slocum stood at the desk for a minute before rapping on the bell. The clerk looked annoyed, but asked, "Yes? What can I do for you?"

"Can I have some hot water sent up to my room?"

"Certainly, sir." He peered at Slocum over the top of rimless glasses. He seemed to be waiting for something, but Slocum said nothing further.

"Do you want to tell me your room number," the clerk asked, "or should I just guess?"

"Twenty-one." Slocum was irritated by the man's supercilious manner. He understood the Hotel Paradise was probably concerned with its image, one that a cowboy covered in trail dust didn't particularly enhance. But rudeness was something he didn't care for. "You have a problem with that?"

"Of course not, sir," the clerk oozed. "A little hot water and soap would probably do you good."

Slocum wanted to punch the little weasel, but there was no point in calling the sheriff down on him. It was going to be tough enough moving around Sterling without getting the law on his ass. "Make that quick, would you?"

"Of course, sir." The clerk hammered a little bell on the desk and Slocum started back up the stairs.

He slipped into the room and slammed the door with more violence than he had intended. Barbara still sat on the edge of the bed. "Anything wrong?"

"That bastard at the desk gets on my nerves."

"He probably thinks you're too uncivilized for his hotel."

"You do too, right?"

"The jury's still out on that one, Mr. Slocum. I try to be open-minded, as long as I can, but . . ."

"I know what you're going to say. Save it."

Barbara said nothing further, and Slocum stared out the window, leaning on the sill with both hands, his head tucked through the lace curtains and out into the heat. The more he thought about the job ahead, the more misgivings he had. But he didn't want Barbara to get discouraged. Keeping his own spirits up was going to be full-time work. If he had to keep her head above water too, they might both drown.

It seemed like an hour before a soft rap on the door signaled the arrival of the hot water. Slocum opened the door and stepped back while two young men, each bearing two sturdy oak pails full of steaming water, moved smoothly and efficiently toward the bathroom. Slocum stood in the doorway while they sloshed the water into the ornate claw-foot tub. When they were finished, the taller of the two kids indicated the tap. "You can add as much cold as you want," he said. "But don't overdo. The hot water line isn't hooked up yet."

Slocum thanked him as the two boys walked to the door, slipped them each a ten-cent piece, then locked the door behind them.

He walked over to the bed and sat beside Barbara. "I'll be back as soon as I can. Will you be alright here by yourself?"

She nodded. "Yes, I'll be alright here by myself."

Slocum stood up. He reached down and took off her hat. She looked up at him, her eyes masked by something. Impenetrably black, they looked as hard as stones. Leaning forward, he kissed her gently on the forehead. The dust and grit made his lips tingle, and he brushed her forehead with one hand, then kissed her again.

Walking slowly to the door, he waited for her to say something. But she didn't. When he opened the door, he looked back, but she wasn't watching him, she seemed to be staring at the carpet. He closed the door quietly, then tried the lock.

He was downstairs and halfway across the lobby when

he wondered whether he should go back. But there seemed to be no reason. Whatever Barbara was thinking, it had nothing to do with him and was nothing she cared to share with him. She needed to be alone, he decided, to sort some things through for herself. What those things were, he could only guess.

Slocum stepped outside into the hot night. The sun was gone, and coal-oil lanterns glowed along the clean street. Horses hitched up and down the street snorted, their hooves clomping on the packed dirt as he passed. He could hear a piano, probably the one Barbara had told him about, long before he spotted the small red-and-white sign announcing the French Quarter.

He stood in front of it for a few moments, taking it in with a wondering shake of his head. Copied from the teeming back streets of New Orleans, the architecture featured wrought iron full of elaborate scrolls and filigrees. Fancy lanterns glowed on either side of the double front doors. The piano tinkled incessantly, and Slocum stepped onto the boardwalk wondering what he would find inside.

As he stepped in, no one paid any attention to him. The place was teeming with cowboys. And with women. A couple of card games—the players concentrating on their hands and bantering good-naturedly—occupied two tables in one corner, opposite the bar. Several of the other tables sported cowboys in threes and fours, a woman or two draped over a shoulder or seated between two men who spoke to one another, dropping hints clearly intended to win the woman's attention.

Slocum had seen dozens of places like it, pretending to be something they only dimly understood, and which their patrons had never seen. Yet McDonald had gone to great pains to create an authenticity that could have gratified no one but himself.

Slocum sat down at one of the few empty tables. A woman in a French peasant costume materialized at his side almost instantaneously. She carried a tray and a pad. "What can I get you, cowboy?" she asked. Slocum was surprised she didn't affect a French accent.

"A beer. A real beer. I don't want yellow dishwater with soapsuds on the top."

"Perish the thought, handsome."

She flounced away, the stiff fabric of her skirt hissing as she walked. Slocum looked around the room. He had the feeling he ought to be looking for something specific and the suspicion that he probably wouldn't recognize it if he saw it.

The woman was back before he completed his survey. She had two beers on the tray, set one in front of him and the other across the table. She pulled a chair out and sat down. "Feel like a little company?" she asked.

"Not especially," he said.

"Not very friendly of you."

"I don't feel very friendly."

"Too bad."

"Why's that?"

She didn't answer. She just smiled and fluttered her eyelids, cocking her head to one side as if the answer should be obvious. It was, in fact, but he was going to string her along a little, let her work a little.

"I don't remember seeing you in here before."

"Never been here before."

"Passing through, or you a new hand?"

"Looking for work, actually."

"I might be able to help you with that."

"You don't look like a trail boss."

"That's the nicest thing anyone's said to me this month."

"Don't mention it."

"No, really, I think I might be able to help you. I know a lot of people around here."

"Why should you help me? You don't even know me."

"Not yet."

"You're pretty sure of yourself aren't you?" Slocum took a long pull on the cold beer. Instead of looking at the woman, he stared at the table.

"What's your name, cowboy?"

"Slocum, John Slocum."

"They call you Jack, I bet. Am I right?"

"Nope."

"My name's Alice. I'm supposed to say Claudette, but I don't think you'd buy that."

"You're right, I wouldn't."

"Do you buy Alice?"

"Why not?"

Alice toyed with her beer, but he noticed she didn't bother to sip it. It was, after all, a prop, and since they both knew it, there was no point in pushing the charade.

"Why don't we find someplace quiet to talk about it?"

"Sure."

She stood up and Slocum downed the rest of his beer before following suit. Alice led the way to winding stairs with a wrought-iron railing at the back of the noisy saloon. Slocum climbed the stairs right behind her, his knees occasionally nudging the ballooning taffeta of her skirt.

At the top of the stairs, Slocum found himself in a dimly lit corridor. It was carpeted in dark red, and his boots made no noise at all as he followed her into the gloom. She stopped in front of a door at the far end of the hall. She opened it quickly and stepped inside. Slocum followed her in, moving cautiously.

A lamp glowed on a table next to the bed. Two chairs completed the furnishings. The place was a lot neater than anything Slocum expected. But it was what it was, and there was no way to disguise the fact.

Slocum closed the door and Alice smiled at him, reaching behind to unhook her dress already. "You don't have to do that," Slocum said.

Alice smiled. "You think I can really get you a job? Are you that green?"

"No."

"Well what, then?" She continued fumbling with the hooks.

"I was hoping you could tell me something about your boss."

Alice stopped smiling. "Well, I can't."

"Why not, are you afraid of him?"

"No."

"Then why?"

She undid the last hook and pulled the dress away. She tossed it on the bed where it landed with a hiss of cloth on cloth. She was naked from the waist up and seemed not at all self-conscious about the fact.

She crooked a finger, gesturing Slocum to come closer.

"Can't you think of anything else to do?" she asked, arching an eyebrow. She cupped her breasts and took a step closer, squeezing them together and rubbing her nipples with extended fingers. "I sure can."

"You work for Kevin McDonald, right?"

She turned away, shaking her head violently from side to side. "No!"

"Alice, I know you do. Why can't you tell me about him?"

"Why should I?"

"Why shouldn't you?"

"Because I work for him, not for you."

"Is that the only reason?"

"Yes . . ." Her voice quavered, and Slocum knew she was lying.

"I don't believe you," he said.

"I don't care what you believe. Get out of here, before I have you thrown out."

"That won't be so easy . . ."

"That's what you think."

Slocum stepped closer. He wrapped his arms around her and realized she was shaking. He rested his chin on her shoulder, whispering in her ear. "Look, you don't have anything to worry about. I can protect you."

"The hell you can. The last girl who bought that line hasn't been seen in almost a year."

"What?"

"You heard me."

"I don't understand."

"You don't have to. All you have to do is go away. I won't tell him about this conversation, and neither will you. That way, we'll both live long enough to forget it ever happened."

"Are you telling me that McDonald would kill you?"

"If he felt like it, yes. If he felt like doing worse, he could do that, too."

"What could be worse?"

Alice laughed bitterly. "He has a place in New Orleans, one that caters to, shall we say, exotic tastes. I don't want to say any more than that. Now please leave . . ."

"I can't," Slocum said. "I have to find someone first, and I'm not leaving until I do."

"You're the one, aren't you. He told us that . . ." She caught herself, but it was too late.

"He told you what?"

"Nothing. Get out, I mean it."

"Where is Liz Holcom?"

"I never heard of her."

"The hell you haven't. Where is she?"

"I don't know."

"Then who does?"

"I don't know."

"Tell me, dammit."

14

Slocum looked at Alice sitting on the bed. She seemed frightened, and Slocum was starting to think that McDonald might be much more than just an angry whoremaster. The terror was genuine, and Slocum didn't know how to get Alice to open up.

"Alice," he begged, "if you tell me what you're afraid of, I can help you."

"No, you can't."

"Is McDonald that powerful?"

"Yes. He has friends, powerful friends. You can't touch him. And if you can't touch him, you can't protect me."

Slocum dropped into a chair and fiddled with his hat. He kept it in his lap and turned it by the brim, around and around and around. He saw his fingerprints in the dust, then looked at his hands. The fingers were smeared with dust slowly turning to dark mud. He realized he was sweating.

"I don't care who his friends are. You can't keep people against their will. Not anymore."

"That's what you think."

"Come with me. I'll get you out of here. I can hide you until I do what I came to do. Then you can leave Sterling. You can leave Colorado, go wherever you want to go."

"Slocum, you know what I am. Where can I go? How can I change what I am? It's too late for me to pretend, to start over, to make my life anything but what it already is."

"That's just not true, Alice. And I have friends, too. I know someone who can help you, get you started on a new life. You've got to trust me. It'll work. I know it will."

She shook her head violently. "No, you can't. I won't

help you. I won't. I wish..." She stopped and looked at him. Her arms folded across her breasts, the tears running down her cheeks, she could have been a fifteen-year-old girl. As he looked closer, he wondered whether she was in fact much older than that.

"At least talk to someone. Maybe a woman..."

"Leave me alone, dammit. Just get out."

Slocum sighed. "I'll make you a deal, Alice. You talk to my friend. Then, if you still don't want to leave here, I'll leave you alone. But you have to promise me you'll at least do that."

He waited for an answer, but it was a long time in coming. "Alright?" he prodded. "Will you do that, at least?"

She seemed to be wavering, and he pushed a little harder, trying to nudge her over the edge. "Please?"

"Alright, alright."

"Okay, I'll meet you tonight. Just tell me where and when."

"I finish at twelve o'clock. You can meet me here?"

"Is that wise? I mean, if you're so afraid of McDonald, maybe it would be better if he didn't know what you were doing."

"Why? Are you afraid?"

"No."

"Then meet me here, behind the hotel at about twelve o'clock."

"I'll be there."

"Sure you will."

Slocum smiled, but she turned away. "Just go now, please..."

He walked to the door quietly. As he turned to pull it closed, Alice looked at him for a second, then looked away. He went down the dimly lit hall, wondering just what he had gotten himself into. It was looking more and more as if McDonald had some hold, not just on the women who worked for him, but on others. Slocum wondered whether McDonald might be blackmailing people of influence, perhaps entrapping them with the connivance of the girls, then holding their dalliance over their heads in order to secure protection for himself and his business.

On the way down the stairs, he watched the patrons in the saloon below. It didn't look all that different from other saloons, except for the expensive decor. But the place seemed to have an atmosphere of malevolence. Despite the clanking piano, the drunken singers joining in from their tables, the French Quarter seemed subdued, as if everyone sensed that something was not quite right. Rather than try to figure out what it was, or run from it, the cowboys seemed to be content to sit there and drink, a little more than normal, and a little less rowdily than usual. In thrall to something they couldn't see or touch, they seemed unable to walk away from it.

Slocum found another empty table and ordered another beer. This time, he discouraged company, and the girl who brought his drink frowned at him, looking back over her shoulder with displeasure. He nursed the beer, watching the other cowboys, the three or four shopkeepers, still in their aprons, having a quiet drink together at one table, and the women, flitting like bees from table to table and man to man, as if they were under some compulsion to make a connection. Slocum wondered whether McDonald might not be putting pressure on the girls, demanding some sort of quota from them, then pushed the thought from his mind. That seemed just too unlikely.

But there was no way to avoid the conclusion that the French Quarter was not the usual whorehouse. And the one man who could be responsible for that difference was its owner, Kevin McDonald. Slocum wondered how he could get a look at the man himself. It would be useful to know what he was up against, but McDonald was not in Sterling, as far as he could tell.

Fifteen minutes later, the beer was almost gone. Slocum was watching the cowboys quietly, almost as if he were invisible. People buzzed around him, coming and going within feet of his table, and yet not one person had looked at him or said hello. There was none of the usual bluster of ranch hands blowing off steam. None of the other girls approached him, as if the word had gone out over some invisible communications system—stay away from that one.

Slocum stood up as a young kid, obviously in his late teens, staggered by, his arm around a brunette old enough to be his mother. The kid bumped him, glanced at Slocum for a second, then turned away. The macho swaggering Slocum expected wasn't there. The kid, if he felt like he had something to prove, was not going to prove it with Slocum. Just one more sign that something was controlling the saloon, something invisible, but very real.

He watched the kid and the brunette thread their way through the crowd and start up the stairs. They were half-way up, Slocum following their progress, when Alice appeared at the head of the stairway. She started down slowly, tripping for an instant and grabbing onto the wrought-iron railing to keep herself from falling.

She stopped, looked around the saloon, spotted Slocum and turned away. But she didn't go back up to the second floor. She averted her eyes, watching her feet as she continued her descent. When she reached the main floor, she looked around expectantly. Slocum noticed something, but he couldn't be sure what it was. He wanted to get a better look, but he couldn't afford to walk up to Alice, not in front of the crowd. She walked toward the bar, keeping her face averted, as if she didn't dare make eye contact with him.

At the bar, a tall, thin rail of a man in a checkered shirt and overalls hooked an arm around her waist and spoke to the barkeep. He grabbed two mugs of beer as soon as they were slapped in front of him, then tugged Alice good-naturedly toward a vacant table. He pulled out a chair for her, in a parody of courtly gallantry, then pressed her down into the chair.

The scarecrow figure of the farmer blocked Slocum's view until the man turned and moved toward a second chair. Now Slocum could see her clearly. And he had been right. An angry welt, already turning blue, had discolored one cheek. Slocum started to get up, but her eyes darted toward him, stopping him in his tracks. Whatever had happened, she did not want to see him. Not then, anyway.

Slocum was puzzled as he left the French Quarter. The streets were almost deserted, and as he walked back toward the hotel, he could hear the piano jangling raucously behind him. At the hotel, he sat on a wooden bench against the front wall for a while. A bit of breeze had kicked up, and dust swirled in the street. Sterling now seemed less peaceful and more sinister. The quiet, instead of something to be relished, was something to make the hair stand up on the back of his neck.

Slocum walked into the deserted lobby and trudged up the stairs. A new clerk had taken his place behind the desk. The new man was a carbon copy of the first, a few years younger, but otherwise indistinguishable. The man glanced at him once, then went back to the newspaper spread on his lap. Slocum walked down the hall to his room with a weight on his shoulders.

He opened the door quietly and stepped inside. A lamp burned dimly on the night table, but the room was empty. "Barbara," he called. When she didn't answer he cursed. "Barbara, where the hell are you?"

Again there was no answer. He sat down on the bed, tapping his feet angrily on the floor, like an irritated teacher trying to decide what to do with the class clown. He heard a noise and turned, jerking the Colt out as he got to his feet. The bathroom door creaked slowly open and Slocum dropped to one knee, bringing the Colt up and aiming at the center of the door.

"Who's there?" he hissed.

Slowly, the door continued to creak, the two-inch band of light beyond it growing to four, then to six. It stopped for a second, then swung the rest of the way in a second, banging against the inside wall.

Barbara McDonough stepped into the open doorway, a towel held in front of her. "Slocum?" she whispered. "Is that you?"

"Jesus," he said, "you scared the hell out of me. Didn't you hear me calling you?"

"I was trying to make up my mind," she said.

"About what?"

"Things. This and that, you know..."

"No," he snapped, "I don't know."

She moved through the doorway, changing from a back-

lit shadow to a golden statue as her skin caught the dim
orange glow of the lamp beside him.

She stepped to the far side of the bed, still holding the
towel up under her chin. It was long enough to cover her
knees, but not wide enough to conceal the curve of her
hips. She looked at him without saying anything. The silence seemed to grow longer and longer, and Slocum didn't
know what to do.

As if she realized it, Barbara took the initiative. She
dropped the towel and lay on the bed. Patting the mattress
beside her, she said, "Come here."

Slocum started to kneel on the bed.

She held up a hand. "Undress first."

Slocum did as he was told. He glanced at the flap of the
saddlebag, still strapped over the wound, but left it in
place. Then he crawled across the bed and lay down, his
head on her stomach.

"I don't know whether I'm making a mistake or not,"
she whispered.

Slocum rolled his head from side to side. "I don't either," he said, his words muffled by the soft mound of her
belly.

"But I decided I don't even care."

Slocum raised himself on his elbows and crawled forward another few inches, then lowered his mouth to kiss
her breasts. He tickled the band of freckles between them
with his tongue. Her nipples were already hard, and he
took one between his teeth, tugging at it playfully, then let
it go and slid along her body like the serpent slithering up
to whisper in Eve's ear.

She wrapped her arms around him, pressing him against
her and spreading her legs wide. Slocum slipped a hand
between them, first caressing the soft fur between her legs,
then opening the moist lips with a finger. Slowly, he
rubbed in a small circle, feeling her grow slippery and
himself grow hard.

"I suppose I am making a mistake," she whispered,
sticking her tongue in his ear.

She slid her own hand between their bodies and curled

cool fingers around him. She stroked it slowly, and he grew harder still. Guiding him toward her, she rubbed her lips with the head of his cock, teasing him with tentative thrusts of her hips, then backing away. He wiggled deeper between her open legs, and she brought him close again, letting his head slide into the dampness. He tensed and she felt the desire coiling in him, let go and raised her hips slowly, taking him in fraction by fraction. He lay there motionless, a coiled spring, letting her control it all.

She moaned softly into his shoulder, her body twisting, the firm breasts flattening against his chest. He could feel her heart hammering against his ribs, the tickle of her breath as she gasped and then, with a surge of wild energy, she rose all the way to meet him, letting her breath out in a long, slow moan. She stretched her arms high over her head and lay back, as if relinquishing control to Slocum.

He started slowly, withdrawing then holding himself steady, poised on the tip of a pyramid, then sliding back down and in. With long, slow strokes, he coaxed her, teased her, until her fingers began to rake his back, goading him to move faster.

Again and again he dove down to the heart of her, digging in with his toes, trying to weld their hips together, then backing away. He was breathing faster now, gasping for air as he ignored the pain in his thigh. Each time, she urged him on, beating her fists against his back. Her hips moved faster, slamming into him again and again and again.

She cried out now, a quavering wail that seemed to fill the room. She spread her legs still wider, grabbing his ass in both hands and pressing him close, as if she wanted to swallow him whole. Their bodies were glued together with sweat that hissed and crackled as their skins peeled away, and the sound spurred them on. The scent of her swirled around him and he could contain himself no longer.

One last time he dove down into her, straining with every muscle, and felt himself spurt again and again, his body quivering with each violent spasm. Spent, he collapsed on her chest, turning to one side to rest his head between her breasts. She stroked his back as he licked her glistening skin. Her heart pounded, a distant echo of the thunder of his own.

He started to get up, but she pressed him back. "Not yet," she whispered. "Not yet."

15

Slocum lay on his stomach. Barbara sat on the bed beside him. She brushed her hair with short, almost vicious strokes. "My hair hasn't been this tangled since . . . well, since I don't know when."

"I don't know why you women all worry so much about tangles," Slocum said, resting a hand on her hip. The skin was cool, smooth. As she jerked the brush again and again, he could feel the play of muscles under his palm.

Ignoring the implicit question, she said, "So, what else did this woman tell you?"

"Alice?"

"Alright, if you insist on being on a first name basis with a slattern, yes, Alice. What else did she say?"

"She said McDonald had friends."

"We all have friends, don't we, Slocum?"

"She meant more than that."

"I know. I'm sorry. I guess I sound like some sort of possessive wife, or something. Yes, he has friends, I'm sure."

"Did Liz tell you anything along those lines?"

"Not in so many words, no."

"But you got that impression from her?"

"Yes, I did."

"Do you know who those friends might be?"

"Not really. After all, I was only here for two weeks or so. If I had heard any of the names, they wouldn't have meant anything to me. I have no idea who's a big wheel and who isn't. Not in Colorado. Not even in Sterling."

Slocum sat up, letting his legs dangle over the edge of the bed. Barbara set the brush down and knelt on the floor beside him. Reaching for one of the strap buckles, she said, "We really ought to take a look at this leg. It could get infected if you're not careful."

"Look, there isn't really much we can do, even if it looks bad."

"Not true. Sometimes, all you have to do is keep a wound clean, maybe drain some fluid off, if it's necessary. Under this leather, it can't breathe, it can't dry out. All you're doing is trapping fluid in there, sweat, God knows what else." She undid the first buckle, letting the strap fall to the floor. When the second buckle came loose, she pulled the strap free from under his thigh and dropped it on the floor next to the first.

Slocum gritted his teeth as she took hold of the leather flap. "Maybe you better let me do that," he said, biting back a pain that wasn't there yet, but would almost surely come any second.

"You men are such babies." Barbara pinched his uninjured leg, grabbing the muscle just above the kneecap.

"Ouch!" he said, slapping her hand away.

He took hold of the leather and started to peel it away from his leg. It caught along one side, and he knew the scab had stuck to the leather. "Wait," Barbara said, "let me take a look."

She bent her head low enough to peek in under the makeshift bandage. "I think you'd better soak that loose," she said. "Maybe you can get it off without breaking it open."

"Not in cold water. No way."

"See, you *are* a sissy."

"Alright, alright. Go ahead. Fill the tub."

Barbara stood, leaning over just far enough to peck at his forehead. He reached up and caught a breast in his hand. She made no attempt to pull away, and he bent his head to plant a kiss on the nipple. She wiggled her hips while he sucked more of the full breast into his mouth. "You're still going to have to soak that leg," she said, finally pulling away.

He watched her walk to the bathroom, grinning broadly. Solid hips and long, muscular legs gave her a seductive

sway, even in so pedestrian a movement. She was not un-
aware and stopped in the doorway to tease him with a full-
length profile, raising one hand high overhead and rubbing
her thigh with the other.

"You better cut that out," Slocum said. "I have to go out
again tonight."

"Just want to make sure you don't get any ideas with
Alice."

"You're starting to sound like Liz. That's the same line
she gave me."

"I'm a fast learner."

"It didn't work, though. Remember?"

She grinned mischievously. "Only because she didn't
give you enough incentive. I think I can handle that part
alright."

"You already have." Slocum laughed. She cocked one
hip, then disappeared. He heard the water start to fill the
tub, and laughed when one long leg appeared in the doorway, bent at the knee, then flexing in an awkward parody
of a French chorus line.

"Where did you ever see something like that?" Slocum
asked.

"St. Louis isn't Paris," she said, "but we do import
things from all over. It's supposed to be the latest rage on
the continent. And, Mister, I'd like to know where *you* saw
it."

"Never mind." Slocum hobbled to the tub and dropped
into the cold water, grateful that it was summertime. He
lay there for a long time, gradually working the piece of
leather loose. When it finally came away, he was glad she
had nagged him. An angry red furrow, coated with dried
blood and full of white and yellow fluid, ran for three
inches from just above his knee in the general direction of
his hip.

Barbara, still naked, hovered in the doorway. She nearly
gagged when she saw the wound, then disappeared from
view. But she was back almost at once, a bottle in one hand
and a ball of soft cloth in the other. She leaned over the
tub, letting her breasts rest on the rim, and poured clear
liquid out of the bottle, sopping the cloth until it dripped

into the water. "What are you doing?" Slocum asked.

"Never mind. Just lie back and hold on. This might hurt."

She pressed the cloth on the wound, squeezing it until he could feel the fluid begin to drain. At the same time, liquid fire flashed across the thigh and shot through his whole leg.

"What the hell . . ."

"Be quiet. It's getting infected."

"Who do you think you are, Clara Barton?"

"Who?"

"Some nurse I knew, during the war. She was half butcher, I think. But you go her one better."

"Hold this." She grabbed his hand and wrapped his fingers around the cloth. The pain had started to subside when she returned with a small jar.

"What's that, now?"

She ignored him. Pulling his hand away, she massaged the ugly scar until she was satisfied it had drained, then smeared a pungent salve, almost as thick as axle grease, and the same color, until she had coated the wound.

"We'll bandage it when you get out. You might as well lie there a bit, until the pain goes away."

She disappeared again. Slocum heard her puttering around in the other room. By the time he climbed out of the tub and dried himself off, she was already dressed and sitting on the bed.

"Where did you get that stuff?" Slocum asked.

"I went to the pharmacist, while you were tart hopping."

"I thought I told you to stay here . . ."

"Don't worry, I wore that silly costume. No one noticed me."

"Are you certain?"

"Yes. And you should be glad I did. That could have turned to gangrene."

Slocum waved his hands to dismiss her concern. "I suppose I should thank you."

"You already did," she said, raising an eyebrow. "Remember?"

"Jesus, is that all you think about?"

"No. But I have four years to make up. Women don't get the chance to express themselves as often as men do. Liz and Alice excepted, of course."

Slocum shook his head. "Stop worrying about Alice. I'm going to bring her back here in a little while, and you're going to have to make friends with her. I have a feeling she knows more than she was letting on. I don't want you antagonizing her. She won't tell us a thing, then."

"I'll be good, I promise."

"What time is it?"

Barbara pulled a pocket watch from her dungarees as Slocum dressed. "Eleven-thirty. What time are you supposed to meet her?"

"She gets off at midnight. I'll come right back here."

"You better take the back stairs."

"What?"

"Don't look at me that way. There is one. I used it. You can't miss it. I'll make sure the door is open."

Slocum stood up and buckled on his gunbelt. He checked the cylinder to make sure it was fully loaded, then slipped the pistol into his holster. He paced nervously for a few minutes, then sat down again.

"You're really worried about what she told you, aren't you?" Barbara asked.

Slocum nodded. "Yeah. Whatever she knows, it was enough to scare her pretty bad. I don't know, maybe she's worried about nothing, but I can't decide that until I know what she's worried *about*."

"Be careful, Slocum." She stepped close and kissed him on top of the head.

Without a word, he stood and walked to the door. "Whatever you do, don't leave the room. And this time I mean it."

Then he was gone.

The hallway was completely dark now. All the lanterns had been extinguished, and he could barely see the wall on either side as he moved toward the stairs. A dull glow at the far end, from a lamp in the lobby, stained the wall at the head of the stairs. He took the steps slowly, glancing around the lobby as he descended. Once he reached the ground floor, he realized the lobby was empty. He walked to the front desk, but the clerk was nowhere in sight. He wondered whether no one was on duty overnight, then decided it didn't make much difference.

The street was just as dark. He glanced up at the front of the hotel and saw light in a couple of windows on the second floor. Far down the street, in saloon row, light spilled out into the night, but all the other shops were dark. Even the sheriff's office, a block away, was unlit.

He kept to the center of the street, looking up at the smear of clouds drifting across the stars. There was a chill in the air, and he shivered. His leg felt much better, and he was glad Barbara had been so adamant about treating it. The tight bandage actually felt good, and the muscles moved freely in his thigh without the tight cincture pressing on the back of his leg.

Slocum turned left alongside a hardware store and moved into an alley that paralleled the street behind a row of shops. It was pitch-black in either direction. The French Quarter was still a hundred yards ahead. Unlike most of the other shops, it was two stories high, and he could see its near wall above the roofs.

When he reached the back of McDonald's place, he found a shallow alcove. He stepped carefully into the small enclosure.

"Alice?" he whispered. "Are you here?"

He heard the rustle of cloth. Turning his head, he leaned into the gloom. "Alice?"

Still no answer. A door creaked open, throwing a pale parallelogram onto the packed earth for a few seconds. It creaked again, then banged home. He heard footsteps on the dirt as he took another step forward. "Alice?"

"Here," she hissed. "Is that you, Slocum?"

He moved quickly, stepping to meet her. She tugged a knit shawl around her shoulders, trying to ward off the chilly night air. "Are you okay?"

She didn't answer, and he reached out to touch her, seeking to reassure her. Again he heard the rustle of cloth.

He was turning to see where it came from when something whistled past his ear. He had ducked instinctively, and the blow caught him on the collar bone. It was hard, and he realized as he fell that it was not a fist. It felt like an ax handle, and he was grateful it had been a glancing blow.

He went to one knee, ignoring the pain in his shoulder. Turning, he was aware that Alice had backed away, tripped over something and fallen to the ground. He slipped sidewise, trying to regain his feet when the second blow caught him high on the back. He went down heavily, landing hard on his face. The wind had been knocked out of him, but he knew he had to move.

Rolling to the side, he slammed into a low wooden step as the club slammed into the dirt just inches away from his head. He heard the unmistakable sound of metal on metal.

Someone had cocked a pistol.

16

The pain stabbed through him like a hot knife. His shoulder ached and he felt trapped. When the gun cocked, he froze for an instant. He felt like a butterfly, waiting for the pin that would fix it forever in one place. Alice screamed and scrambled out of the darkness. She stepped over him as he tried to rise. Tripping, she stumbled forward as the gun went off.

Slocum hauled the Colt Navy out and struggled to free himself from the lacy prison of Alice's gown. He heard her whimpering and scrambling away. The gun went off again, its report thunderous in the confined alcove.

Slocum was on his feet now, and the gunman backed away. He was nothing more than a dark blob, blotting out the starlight behind him. Slocum grabbed for the shadow's extended arm, but the man eluded him, and he fell head-long over Alice's extended leg.

The man started to back up. He pulled the trigger again, but the hammer landed with a dull thud. Either he was out of ammunition or he had a bad shell. Either way, it seemed to panic him and he turned to run down the alley. Slocum chased after him, his bad leg hampering his progress. At the end of the alley, the man darted into the open for an instant, then disappeared behind the corner of a low shed.

Slocum hobbled around the corner, but the man was widening the gap. "Stop, you sonofabitch," Slocum shouted. He cocked the Colt and the man skidded to a halt. There was no cover, and he knew he'd never make it to the front corner of the shed.

Skipping on the bad leg, Slocum held the Colt out in front of him and closed to within five feet.

"Who the hell are you?" Slocum demanded.

"Go to hell."

Slocum slashed him across the shoulder with the Colt, raking the thin flesh over the collar bone with the front sight. The man clapped a hand over the shoulder and spat at him.

"Nice manners," Slocum said. "But you're still gonna tell me your name."

The man shook his head, and Slocum raised the Colt a second time.

"Go ahead, you bastard."

Instead, Slocum prodded him with the pistol. "Let's go," he said.

The man tried to resist, but Slocum slipped in behind him and pressed the muzzle of the Colt against the base of his spine. "You want to keep on walking, you better move, cowboy."

"Don't do that, man. Just don't do that. It might go off."

"It might at that," Slocum chuckled. "Course, if it does, it won't bother me in the least. Now move." He cracked the muzzle sharply against a vertebra, and the man nearly fell in his haste to comply.

"I'm going, I'm going."

At the rear of the shed, the man paused. "Which way?" he asked. His voice trembled just a little.

"Back the way we came," Slocum hissed. "And don't even think about trying to run, because I will shoot you as sure as you're standing there. Do you understand?"

They moved down the alley without speaking. Alice raced toward them, and Slocum sighed with relief. "Are you alright?"

She shook her head. "Yes," she said, swallowing hard. "I'm alright."

"I thought you'd been shot."

"I didn't want to shoot nobody," the gunman said. "Honest to God. I wasn't supposed to."

"What do you mean, supposed to? Were you *told* to do this?"

"I didn't say that."

"You might as well have."

"Unh, unh. No, sir. Nobody told me to do nothing."

"Then what were you doing there?"

"Nothing."

"I suppose you usually wait around behind the French Quarter, just to see what sort of excitement turns up. Is that it?"

"Yeah." Slocum rapped him hard across the base of the spine. "I mean, no. I mean, I . . . you know, I just happened to be there, that's all."

"And what were you trying to do?"

"Nothing. Just scare you a little, that's all."

"I see, it's just a prank, is it?"

"A what?"

"Never mind," Slocum barked. "Alice, you ever see him before?"

"Once or twice, yes. But I don't know him. I mean, he came into the saloon two or three times. That's the only place I've ever seen him."

"What about friends, you ever see him with anybody else?"

"Not really. Other ranch hands, I guess. No one I know, though. They all look pretty much alike, to me."

"Funny," the man said, "that's what they say about whores, too."

Slocum rapped him again, harder this time. "I think you better apologize to the lady."

"Lady?" The man snorted. Slocum recocked the Colt, and the man started to turn.

"Alright, alright. I'm sorry."

"Ma'am. I'm sorry *ma'am*. You got that?"

"Yes, sir. I'm sorry, ma'am."

"Now turn around." The man did as he was told and Slocum popped a wooden match with his thumbnail. The head flared, and the man backed away as the flame danced on the end of the stick. "Just want to get a good look at you. You know why?"

"Unh, unh."

"Well, I'm gonna tell you. If I ever see you again, I'm going to shoot you. You understand?"

"Yes, sir."

"And I mean it. You can tell that to whoever hired you, and then you better look for some other town. Because I'm gonna be around for a while. And Sterling just isn't that big. If you're here, I *will* see you. And I *will* shoot you."

The man started to back away. When Slocum made no attempt to stop him, he started to move even faster. Twenty feet away, he turned and ran as fast as he could. In a moment, all they could see was the light-colored band around his hat. A second later, there was nothing but retreating footsteps to remind them he'd been there at all.

"Now," Slocum said, "I wonder what the hell that was all about."

"I told you McDonald had friends. He must have known I was going to meet you."

Slocum looked at her closely. He remembered the bruise he had seen early. It was all but invisible now under a thin coat of powder and rouge. "What happened to your face?" he asked.

"Nothing."

"Don't lie."

"I'm not lying, damn you."

"Alright, come on. We better get out of here, just in case the cowboy decides to come back."

"Where can we go?"

Alice was on the verge of panic, and Slocum shushed her with a finger to her lips. "It'll be alright. I'll take you to someone. We have a room at the hotel."

"What hotel?"

"The Paradise."

"No, I don't want to go there. *I won't.*"

"Alice, get ahold of yourself."

"You poor dumb bastard," she said.

Slocum was out of patience. He took her roughly by the arm and started to drag her along. She struggled at first, but realized she couldn't break free. Reluctantly, she fell in step beside him. Slocum kept one hand just above her elbow. "Hurry," he said.

She laughed, but said nothing.

At the rear of the hotel, he found the back entrance

Barbara had told him about. He opened the door quietly and stepped into the bottom of a pitch black well. Still holding onto Alice, he pulled her in after him. When the door closed behind her, it was impossible to see. Slocum lit a match and found a set of dusty stairs just three feet from where he stood.

He let his hand slide down Alice's forearm, then gripped her curled fingers in his own. It was she who applied all the pressure now, squeezing as if she were afraid he would let go. Carefully, feeling his way with blind feet, he took the steps one at a time.

There was a landing halfway up, and he had to light another match. The stairway turned to the left and continued on up. He could hear Alice in the dark, her breathing the shallow gasps of a person in abject terror. Almost unconsciously, she started to pull him back, her hand tugging his as if to retard the ascent.

"Why are you doing this?" she whispered at him. In the dark, her voice startled him. It sounded like the hiss of a startled snake, and he shuddered.

"I'll explain later," he said. "Be quiet."

She pulled his arm a little harder, but said nothing.

Slocum bumped into something with his shoulder. Groping in the dark, he found rough wood under his fingers. To the left, he found a corner, then the smoother surface of a door panel. He lit a third match, found the knob, and let go of her hand to grab the knob before shaking the match out.

The knob felt rough under his fingers, as if it were rusty, and when he turned it, the latch creaked. But the door opened. Just to the left, he saw the dull glow of the lobby lantern. It took his eyes a few seconds to adjust, even to the pale illumination. He pushed the door all the way open, using his weight to muffle the creaking hinges.

Stepping into the hallway, he pulled Alice through after him, then closed the door. "Come on," he whispered.

He stepped carefully on the carpeted floor. He knew about where the door to their room was, but moved slowly, unwilling to risk making any sound at all. Almost at the end of the corridor, he lit a fourth match. The door to twenty-one was five feet away.

And it was wide open.

Slocum cursed under his breath.

"What's wrong?" Alice asked.

"Nothing. Come on."

He moved quickly now, stepping into the room and half dragging Alice in after him. He called softly, "Barbara?"

Something was wrong. Even if she had ignored his injunction to stay in, she would not have left the door wide open. He stepped to the right, pulling Alice along, then tugged her down as he dropped to one knee.

Leaning close, he could smell her perfume, more delicate than he would have thought. He found her ear with his lips. "Lie on the floor and don't move until I say so."

She inhaled sharply, ready to ask a question, but he pressed a finger to her lips. "Ssshhh . . ." he said. With his hand on her back, he guided her to the floor. Then he rolled as far to the right as he could. He drew the Colt and started to crawl. He remembered where the bathroom door was and groped for it with one hand, keeping his balance with the other.

The Colt thumped against a doorframe, then slid noiselessly through the open doorway. He crawled through the doorway and stood up. He lit a match, but the bathroom was empty. A small lamp stood on a windowsill, and he lit it, just as the match burned down to his fingertips.

Turning the lamp all the way up, he lay on the floor and pushed it through the open doorway. As his eyes adjusted, he could see that the room was empty.

Barbara was gone.

Slocum stepped into the main room, a puzzled look on his face.

"Can I get up now?" Alice asked.

Slocum nodded.

"I told you . . ." she said.

17

Slocum set the lamp on the table. Alice stood by the door, trembling.

"We have to get out of here," she said.

"Not until you tell me everything you know. I am through playing games with you. You know something, and you're going to tell me."

"Or what?" Some sudden fire flared up in her, a spirit she had not previously demonstrated. "What are you going to do, beat me? Kill me?"

Slocum waved in disgust. "That's bullshit, Alice. I don't do that sort of thing."

"You're a man, aren't you? That's what men do. That's how they handle women."

"Not this man. Maybe that's how McDonald treats you. But if it is, then you have all the more reason to tell me what you know."

"No! He'll kill me if he finds out I spoke to you."

"He already knows, Alice." Slocum raised his voice. He was getting angry at her pigheadedness, but didn't know how to handle her. "He knows because you already told him. Didn't you?"

She turned away from him.

"Dammit, answer me," Slocum shouted. "You told him, didn't you?"

"Yes, I told him. I had to. You saw my face. You saw that bruise. It would have been a lot worse if I hadn't told him what he wanted to know."

"And you think he'll leave you alone now? Is that what you think?"

"He will. I helped him. He owes me."

"That's where you're wrong, Alice. He doesn't owe you. He *owns* you. As long as you keep giving in to his threats, you're his. The only way to get out from under him is to prove that you can stand on your own two feet. To prove that he can't intimidate you anymore. That's the only thing men like McDonald understand."

"What the hell do you know about it? What do you know about anything? Slocum, the only thing I have is my looks—my face and my body. If he takes them away from me, I have nothing. Who's going to pay a woman with scars all over her face? You, would you pay for that, Slocum?"

"It's not that simple."

"Oh, but it is that simple. There is no choice here, Slocum. None. I have what I look like. That's what I sell, that's how I stay alive. He takes that away, I might as well be dead."

"Dammit, Alice. You *let* him keep you down. And if you keep on *letting* him, you might as well be dead."

"If I cross him, I *will* be, Slocum. You and I both know that."

"No. I can protect you."

"Like you protected your girlfriend? Is that what you can do for me, Slocum? Is that how you plan to protect me? And do I have to go to bed with you for that?"

"No, you know better than that."

"Slocum, I know all there is to know about men. And there's only one thing worth knowing. Do what they want, and they treat you nice. Don't, and they don't. Hell, Slocum, the only difference between me and a married woman is the ring. We both sell ourselves. I do it for money, she does it for a roof over her head. At least I get to choose my own roof."

"Do you, Alice? Is that what you call it, choosing?"

"To hell with you."

"Where is Liz Holcom?"

"I don't know."

"Yes, you do. You might as well help me, because I'm going to find her. I can do it with or without you. But I promise you one thing, if I do it without you, I'm going to tell McDonald you helped me."

"You wouldn't do that . . ."

"Why not? Why shouldn't I? If anything happens to Liz and the others, you're going to pay for it. I can guarantee you that."

"So I can't win, can I? If I help you, he'll kill me, and if I don't, you'll sign my death warrant. It amounts to the same thing, either way."

"It doesn't have to. You can help. And if you do, I promise he won't hurt you. I'll see to that."

"What are you going to do, kill him? Because that's what you'll have to do. And he has powerful friends, Slocum, men who can buy and sell a hundred like you."

"Not really. There *is* no one like me. You can't buy a man like me, no matter how much money you have. I'm not for sale."

"No? And what did Liz do for you? Money isn't the only currency, Slocum. Not when you're buying a man's soul."

Slocum sat on the bed. He shook his head in exasperation. Alice took a step toward him, then stopped. "Look, Slocum," she said. "Why can't you see how it really is? McDonald gets what he wants, always. It's always been that way, and it always will be. Some things, you just can't fight."

She took another step and reached out to him. "Look," she said, "I'd help you if I could. But I have to think about myself first. I'm all alone in this. You have your reasons for doing this, and I have to understand that. But you have to allow me my reasons."

Slocum took her hand. "Sit down," he said, tugging gently. He let go and patted the mattress. "Alice, look, I won't make you do anything you don't want to do. But I need help. I know you are frightened, but you can't let that stop you. Just tell me everything that happened since I saw you this afternoon."

Alice lowered herself, almost primly, tucking her skirt under her, then pressing it between her legs as she sat. "I hate this," she said. "I just hate it."

"Take your time."

"Someone saw you," she said. "This afternoon, some-one saw you at the French Quarter. They were watching, and when you left, one of McDonald's men followed you back here. Kevin came to my room, and he wanted to know why you were here. He said you killed two of his people, and he wanted to know what you were doing here. I told him I didn't know. And he . . ."

"That's when he hit you?"

She nodded "He told me he wouldn't hurt me, but he wanted to protect himself. He said you were a threat, that you were after him for some reason."

"Did he tell you why?"

"He said it was personal, that it was something between you and him. He didn't say what."

"So what did you tell him?"

"I said that you were looking for Liz. That's all I told him. I . . ." She broke off in sobs.

Slocum waited patiently. The sobbing trailed off, and she took a deep breath. "I told him you were coming back, coming to meet me tonight. That's all, I swear, that's all I told him."

"And did he say anything else?"

"No."

"Did he say anything about Liz and the others?"

"What others? I didn't know there were any others in-volved."

Slocum shook his head. "Three others. Three women he lured out here. He wanted to put them to work, and Liz helped them get away. They almost made it, too, but he sent a mob after them. He caught Liz and two of the other women, girls, really."

"You said there were three others."

"That's right. Barbara got away when they jumped the wagon. She came back with me, back here."

She looked at him sharply. "You mean she was here, in this room? And that's why he didn't care that you were coming back. He wanted her, Barbara you said, he wanted her back. And he figured that either she would be with you at the hotel or she would wait here. Either way, he could get to her."

"That's right," Slocum said.

"So he used me as bait."

"Yes. And I have to find those girls. They'll never get away again without help. In the meantime . . . well, I guess I don't have to tell you what will happen."

"No," she said sadly, "you don't."

"If you know where they are, you have to tell me. Even if you just have an idea. Anything at all that might help, you have to tell me. I don't have much time."

Alice stood up and walked to the door. Slocum watched her carefully, convinced she was going to leave. And he knew he wasn't going to stop her. Instead, she turned back to face him. She leaned against the door, her hands folded behind her.

"I don't know what I can do to help," she said. "I mean, I want to, but . . ."

"Anything you can tell me. Anything at all."

"I heard something. I don't know whether it means anything or not. I don't even know whether it's true. It's just . . ."

"Never mind, just tell me."

"Kevin is part owner of the Sterling Railroad Development Corporation."

"But there's no railroad here," Slocum said.

"Yes, there is. It's not operational. But the tracks are almost all in. It runs to Denver. And they plan to build a northern line, too, up to Cheyenne."

"I don't understand what you're getting at."

"He has this idea. You've seen those fancy railroad cars, the kind rich people have. Their own cars, they just hook on and go wherever they want to?"

Slocum nodded.

"Well, Kevin, he . . . Kevin plans to put the French Quarter on wheels. I guess that's the easiest way to say it."

"A whorehouse on wheels?"

Alice nodded. "He's supposed to have the cars, two of them, already. But, that's all I know. It's just something I heard. I don't even know if it's true. Liz was telling me about it one day, but she never finished. And she was always telling stories anyway, so I didn't pay much attention. The next time I saw her, she didn't mention it, and I didn't believe her anyway, so I didn't ask."

"Where's the railroad line here? Where does it run?"

"I don't know." She held a handkerchief in her hands and stopped talking while she uncoiled the tight rope she had made of it. "That's all, I swear."

"Alright, alright. Who would know?"

"I don't know. No one. I . . ."

"What about the other girls at the Quarter?"

"No, I don't think so. Besides, you can't get them in trouble. You can't talk to them. You . . ."

"But I have to find those cars."

"You don't know that that's where they are."

"But I don't know they're *not* there, either. And I don't have anyplace else to look."

Alice took a step away from the door. "But, Slocum, you . . ." she was saying when she suddenly flew toward him. He thought she was about to attack him when he realized the door had been thrown open behind her. Before he could draw his Colt, three men stood just inside the door. Slocum saw their drawn weapons and raised his hands.

Alice struggled to get up from the floor, and Slocum put out a hand to help her.

"Leave her there," the man in the middle said.

Slocum looked at the intruders. He had never seen any of them before, but the short man in the middle looked vaguely familiar. But he couldn't place the face.

"You just rest easy, son," the little man said. "Cal, grab ahold of that colt, would you?"

Cal, a gangling kid not yet out of his teens, stepped toward Slocum, making sure he didn't come between him and the little man's gun. He stepped around the bed and reached across from behind to jerk the Navy out of Slocum's holster.

"Who the hell are you?" Slocum demanded.

"Shut up! On your feet, cowboy." He jerked his pistol in a vicious arc, and Slocum stood, keeping his hands at shoulder level. "Cal, hog-tie the sonofabitch." He grinned at Slocum. "You give me a reason, cowboy. Just give me a reason."

Slocum looked at Alice, but she shook her head as if to say she had no idea who the little man was.

But the little man took care of the mystery himself. "You left my brother out there with a hole in his chest, you bastard. And when this is over, you'll have one of your own."

Now Slocum knew where he'd seen the face. It was that of the man Barbara had killed at the ravine.

"I don't know what you're talking about."

The little man moved too fast for him, catching Slocum on the point of the chin with the pistol. He tripped over the bed as he ducked back, and then fell to the floor.

The heavy boot put him out altogether.

18

The blindfold was giving Slocum a headache. The hard knot of cloth at the base of his skull kept boring into him, no matter how he twisted or turned. The creaking of the wagon was monotonous, and his captors had exchanged fewer than a dozen words since the trip started. Gagged, he was unable to ask Alice if she was alright, or even if she was there.

He'd been in deep holes before, but it had been a long time since he'd been in one this deep. It was impossible to mistake the smoldering rage in the little man's eyes. That he meant to avenge his brother was beyond doubt. That he would make Slocum pay was the only thing on the little man's mind. But that was just part of the problem. Saddled with Alice, a house of cards to begin with, and now, no doubt, all but ready to collapse in the first breeze, he was handicapped beyond measure.

As he lay there in the wagon bed, his arms and legs half numb from the tight ropes binding them together, he wondered how in hell he had managed to get himself in so deep with so little reason. A thousand dollars was nothing to sneeze at, but he hadn't expected to work so hard to earn it. He cursed himself for being just a little too greedy, or a little too chivalrous. Maybe both.

But, whatever his reasons, he had badly miscalculated. There could be no two ways about that. Thinking it through from the beginning, he wondered whether he had let a raised skirt turn his head. But he had agreed to help Liz before she paid him the visit on the hill. Barbara was not even a lecherous gleam in his eye when he had sold his services to the first bidder. So what the hell was it? he wondered. How did he manage to shoot himself in the foot so easily? And why?

He wanted to laugh, but his head hurt too much. The pain would serve him right, he thought, but somehow it didn't seem atonement enough to even the score. He was going to have to pay dearly for this one. And even while he served as his own judge and jury, he knew what his defense had to be. He had tried to help a woman who appeared to need it. Just how accurate that assessment might be was beyond dispute at this point. The only remaining question seemed to be whether he could make good on his promise.

On that, the jury had been deliberating for far too long. It did not look good. That he was a fool now seemed a fair indictment. All that remained to be determined was the penalty. Was charity a hanging offense? Something told him in Colorado it just might be.

The wagon tilted sharply, and Slocum slid toward the tailgate. They were heading uphill, and their pace slowed, either because the trail was treacherous or because they were in alien terrain. His feet slammed into the tailgate, sending a shock all the way up his spinal column to detonate in his brain. He knew he groaned because he could feel his throat contort, the muscles grow taut and then slacken. But he heard nothing.

They had been traveling for nearly three hours, as far as he could tell, but how the hell do you gauge time trussed up like a market pig in the back of a wagon? He rolled to the side and felt something soft with the tips of his fingers. He braced his feet, pushed himself even farther to the right, and his fingers sank into a tangle of smooth cloth. He couldn't move his hands or arms much, but hoped he'd found Alice there beside him. If he could get free, at least he wouldn't have yet another hostage to worry about.

He struggled with the ropes, but his arms were so tightly bound the slightest movement set his shoulder joints on fire. Moving his legs was useless. There was nothing to rub the rope against, and he couldn't see a damn thing anyway. For all he knew a straight razor might be lying right beside him.

Slocum tried to sit up, not knowing why, but convinced

he had nothing to lose. He struggled to keep his balance nearly sitting on his hands. But he no sooner managed to get himself upright when the wagon plunged over the edge and started downhill. He slammed back into the wagon bed. When his head struck the hard wood, the knotted cloth felt like a bullet slamming into his skull. He lay there gasping, seeing false light flashing before his eyes. He wanted to curse, but the muffled grunt he managed was too humiliating.

The wagon seemed out of control, picking up speed as it plunged down a long incline, and he thought for a minute they had simply cut it loose, let it roll on its own, to break apart on stones far below, tearing him and Alice to pieces in the process.

But the brakes squealed, and the wagon slowed a little, reluctantly at first, then more abruptly. And he heard the men in front for the first time in more than an hour.

"Jesus Christ, Cal, where the hell'd you learn to drive a wagon?"

"Never did learn, Roy."

"You're kidding."

And that was the extent of the exchange. The wagon continued on, at a more deliberate pace now, as if the men weren't sure where they were going. Then he realized it might still be dark. They might be looking for something or someone in the pre-dawn.

Then Cal spoke again. "Roy, you sure we're headed right?"

"Just drive, dammit."

The wagon jolted over some rough ground, tossing Slocum mercilessly back and forth. After another fifteen or twenty minutes, the wagon slowed again. This time, it rolled slowly to a halt. Slocum heard someone jump down from the wagon, then the creak of hinges several yards away. The wagon lurched again, and then the hinges creaked one more time, followed by the slam of closing doors.

The canvas was ripped away from the rear end of the wagon and hands grabbed him by the ankles. He felt himself being pulled from the wagon. Expecting to land on his back, he braced himself for the impact, but whoever was dragging him dropped his feet, and he tilted forward. He still landed heavily, but at lest it was upright.

His blindfold was whipped off, and he blinked against a bright band of light slashing across the floor a few feet in front of him. He blinked away the blurred film covering his eyes and realized he was in an old barn. The floor was littered with dry straw, and the place stank faintly of horses.

He turned to the wagon and saw Alice lying against the side panel. She was blindfolded and tied in the same way he was. Cal reached in and grabbed hold of the rope around her ankles, pulling her close enough to lift her out of the wagon. He set her down and removed her blindfold. She stared at Slocum, her eyes wide with fright. Her head swiveled from side to side, and she seemed to be trying to say something, but the gag made a jumble of her words.

"Where the hell are we?" Slocum tried to ask behind his gag.

Cal looked at him for a moment, then walked away, leaving him and Alice to stare at one another in mute bewilderment. Roy was nowhere to be seen. Slocum heard the door open again, and he jumped on bound legs to one side trying to look through the open door. He caught a brief glimpse of tall peaks in the distance and a rolling meadow full of daisies in the foreground just before the door swung shut again.

As far as he could tell, they were alone in the barn.

Slocum bounced over to Alice and dropped to his knees. He turned his back to her, leaning his head toward her hips, and she finally understood that he wanted her to tug the gag free. If they were to have a chance to get out of this mess, he would need to tell her what to do. Her fingers fumbled with the knot, but it wouldn't give. Unable to move her arms, she couldn't get the necessary grip. Slocum turned his head farther, and she raked at the cloth with her fingertips, finally working it away from his jaw. Twisting his head while she continued to claw at the tight band of fabric, he managed to get it away from his mouth. He spat out a wad of cloth and was able to breathe decently for the first time in hours.

Roy was coming back. Slocum knew that as surely as he knew his own name. He didn't know when, but he knew for sure the little man wouldn't stay away too long. Slocum looked around the barn, desperately searching for something to cut the rope around his wrists. Anything, a saw, an old plow, something that could part it a strand at a time or all at once, it didn't matter. He just knew he had to get the rope off before Roy returned, or he was a dead man.

But there was nothing. The barn hadn't been used in a long time, and virtually anything of any utility had long since been removed. Slocum hauled himself to his feet, bracing himself on the tailgate and using it to lever himself up. It was slow going, and the muscles in his neck and shoulders felt as if they were tearing away from the bone.

He was almost there when the door hinges squeaked again. He heard footsteps on the brittle straw, and Roy appeared around the corner of the wagon.

"Well, well, well, cowboy, I see you managed to get yourself a little air. But that's alright, I was gonna take that muzzle off anyhow. I got a few questions to ask you."

"What the hell is going on?"

"I said *I* had a few questions. Now you just mind your manners and tell me what I want to know. If I don't ask you nothing, don't say nothing. When I ask you a question, you just answer it, understand?"

"Go to hell."

"Now listen, old son, it don't make no difference to me if I gut you now or shoot you later. You understand me? You sass me, I might as well put you away. I'm gonna do it anyhow, and I don't give a damn when. The man wants to know something, but if you don't know or if you do, he don't know. Now, I can cut your throat right here and tell him you don't know nothing. It don't matter to me. Not at all."

"But it matters to me, Roy . . ."

Roy jerked his thead around, and Slocum leaned forward to see who had spoken.

A tall man, who might have been handsome if it had not been for a slightly porcine cast to his features, stepped into view. His bright red hair and generous freckles were set off by a full ginger mustache and a pair of bright blue eyes, like glacial ponds seen from a high peak.

"I was just starting to soften him up," Roy said. He stammered a bit, and Slocum realized he was frightened of the red-haired man.

"So I heard. You were saying something about not being overly concerned with whether or not Mr. Slocum, here, knew anything at all, weren't you?"

"Well, I was just . . ."

"Roy, I know what you were doing. And I told you, mind your p's and q's. I want information, not vengeance."

"I know that. But, sometimes you have to frighten somebody first, you know? Put the fear of God into him, before . . . ."

"You mean the fear of Roy, don't you?"

"No, I swear, Mr. McDonald, I didn't . . ."

"Get out of here."

So, Slocum thought, this was the famous Kevin McDonald. The red-haired man watched Roy leave the barn. Only when the door closed again did he turn to his prisoner. "Well, Mr. Slocum, I see you're rather predictable."

"Where's Liz Holcom? Where's Barbara McDonough?"

"They're fine, Mr. Slocum. Don't you worry your head about them. Karen and Mabel are fine, too. And they'll continue to be fine as long as you cooperate."

"Cooperate? What the hell does that mean?"

"Oh, I think you know very well what that means, Mr. Slocum. You have something of mine. Or you know where it is. And I want it back."

"I don't know what you're talking about."

"Oh, but I think you do."

"The only thing of yours I had you already got back. That was four women who were no more yours than the coffin belongs to the dead man."

"Is that some sort of veiled threat, Mr. Slocum?"

"Not at all. I just meant that you don't own those women, no matter what you think."

"This is not about women, Mr. Slocum. This is about money. Quite a lot of money, actually."

"Sorry, I can't help you there, Kevin."

"Perhaps not. But let me at least go through the motions, alright?"

"Fire away."

"Liz Holcom helped herself to twenty-five thousand dollars of my money. I want to know where it is."

Slocum was stunned. This was two and a half times the amount Liz had claimed she had in the wagon, and some of that was his own. Slocum wavered just a bit, but McDonald had a keen eye.

"So, I see that sum means something to you, eh?"

"When you make a living the way I do, it sure as hell does. I've never seen that much money in my life. Yours or anybody else's."

"Come, now, Mr. Slocum. Surely you don't expect me to believe that?"

"It's the truth."

"I see."

"I'd be happy to help you look for it, though. Provided you let the women go."

McDonald laughed. "You must think I'm a fool, Mr. Slocum. But I'm not, you see. Those women are my collateral, so to speak. If I don't find the money, they will have to earn it back, twice over. Once to replace the missing funds, and again as, shall we say, punitive damages."

"No deal, Kevin."

"But I'm not offering to deal, Mr. Slocum. I don't have to. I hold all the cards. And there are other ways to elicit information."

He lashed out with an open palm, striking Slocum in the chest and sending him reeling backward. He collapsed in a heap, and McDonald smiled at him. Then, almost as quickly as he had shoved Slocum, he grabbed the front of Alice's dress and jerked it away. Reaching out with one finger, he dimpled the flesh of one breast. Turning to Slocum, he said, "They're quite lovely, aren't they? For now..."

Then he turned away. Slocum lost sight of him almost immediately. But he could hear McDonald's boot heels on the packed earth of the barn floor.

"Think it over, Mr. Slocum. When I come back, I'll not be in a very forgiving mood."

19

The door slammed and Slocum looked at Alice. She looked so helpless with the remnants of her dress dangling down around her waist. A bright red circle marked the point where McDonald had dug his finger into her flesh. Her eyes were like saucers, and the tears ran down her cheeks, dribbling over her chin and landing on her breasts, where they sparkled in the band of sunlight coming through an open loft door high above them.

Rather than getting to his feet, Slocum started to creep across the floor like an inch worm, lying on his back and bending his knees repeatedly to dig his heels into the dirt floor. He crawled away from the sunlight into the shadows, looking for anything he could use to saw through the ropes.

His wrists chafed under the ropes, and his palms scraped painfully over the floor, but there was no other way to move. In one corner of the barn, he maneuvered around a shaky partition into a small room. In the dim light it was hard to see anything clearly. Shapes dangled from one wall, light gray shadows among the black, but he couldn't tell if anything on the wall would help him.

He crept closer, his eyes straining to pierce the gloom. It looked as if some garden tools leaned against the wall in one corner, but he couldn't be sure. The closer he came, the higher his hopes soared, and the faster his heart beat. He thought he could hear it like a small drum echoing in the closed space. He bumped into the corner headfirst and knocked something over. A long wooden handle lay across his chest, and he twisted to see what it was. It was a rusty hoe, its blade dulled beyond use. He twisted away from it and spun around to see what else he could find. He used his legs to knock over two more tools, a rake and a spade. The rake was useless, and the spade, its pointed blade worn away to a smooth, straight edge, was nearly so.

He tried to be quiet, letting the implements strike his body, and nearly hitting himself in the eye with the spade handle in his haste. Then, high on the wall, he spotted something that made his heart stop. Resting there, hung on a wooden peg, was a sickle. It was rusty like the other tools, but the edge might be sharper. But how the hell could he reach it? He couldn't use his hands, and it was too high to knock off with his head.

He squirmed around on the floor, until he lay parallel to the hoe. Using his feet to press on the blade, he got the handle up high enough to slide his shoulder under it. Sitting up, with the handle balanced on his collar bone, he bent his legs to bring all his weight down on the blade. The handle rose almost vertically, but when he relaxed, it started to topple back toward him. He tried again and still couldn't overcome gravity. But the third time, he slammed his heels hard onto the rusty metal and the hoe sprang up and over, tipping into the corner and staying put.

Slocum swung around now, pivoting on his tailbone, and levered himself up along the wall. He was halfway home. The sickle dangled above him like a rusty moon, eighteen inches over his head. Bending at the waist, he bit into the handle of the hoe. The heavy wood hurt his teeth, and the balance was all wrong on his first try. The weight of the hoe pried his jaws open and he lost control. He bent over farther, nearly losing his own balance, but managed to grip the handle again with his teeth.

Painfully, he raised the hoe handle along the wall, nudging the sickle blade to knock it loose. It swung back and forth like a pendulum, but it stayed put. Again he bumped it and again it dangled. But it didn't fall.

This time, he jerked his head up and the handle caught under the blade. Biting deeper into the wood, he tried to keep the handle vertical and backed away from the wall. The sickle slid forward and uphill on its peg, teetered for a moment, then fell into the jumbled tools in the corner.

Slocum held his breath, praying no one had heard the dull clang of the blades jangling together.

When it seemed no one had, he slid back down the wall and turned his back, feeling with his fingers for the sickle. It took him a while to find it, but when he tried to pull it free, it caught on something. Slocum cursed quietly. He had no leverage at all with his arms, and his fingers couldn't generate enough pull on their own. He tried twisting and tugging within the inch or so of movement the rope permitted. His shoulder sockets felt as if they were on fire.

He had no choice but to risk another racket. Closing his fingers over the sickle, he gritted his teeth and rolled over, pulling more tools over on top of him. The heavy wooden handles slammed into his arms and back, but his body muffled the sound and the sickle was his.

Crawling away from the corner, he backed against the partition and traced the curve of the blade with his fingertips. He could feel the gritty rust clinging to the blade, but its edge was still there. It was pitted here and there on the inner curve, but it just might do. But how the hell could he use it and hold it at the same time?

He found the handle and backed away from the partition enough to squeeze the sickle in lengthwise. McDonald had said he'd be back in an hour. Already, it seemed that more than half that time had expired. Slocum broke out in a cold sweat as he maneuvered the sickle up against the partition, then leaned back, trying to drive the point into the wood deep enough to hold it. It slipped away, and he nearly lost his grip on the sickle. He tried again, probing at the wood with the blunt pointed end. Again and again, he pecked at the wood, and again and again it sank in a fraction of an inch, then stopped.

Once more, he tried, sliding along the partition a bit, until he found a knothole in the rough lumber. The point went in more than an inch, then stopped. He leaned back, putting all his weight on the handle, and the blade sank in a little more.

Bracing it against the small of his back, he stretched his hands back along its length, then brought his hands down on either side of the sickle blade. He could feel the gritty rust against the heels of his hands, the cold metal beneath it, and, with his fingertips, the dirt below. Slowly, he started to saw back and forth, stopping every few strokes to make sure the sickle was secure. He heard a few strands pop, and he started to saw harder, pressing down, forcing the rope against the rusty, ragged edge of the blade. The strands parted with soft snaps, and he tried to pull his hands apart. He couldn't feel the rope with his fingers.

More strands gave, but it was slow going. Because the rope was coiled several times around his wrists, he couldn't bring any real pressure to bear on the cut. He stopped to listen, but still heard nothing. The rough blade was scraping the skin off his hands, but he kept on, sawing and tugging, sawing and tugging.

The rope continued to give, but only grudgingly. His hands were slippery with blood now, trickles running down between his fingers. Fibers from the rope stuck to his bloody skin and he sawed even faster. Then, with a final snapping sound, like a small twig, the rope parted. He felt its severed ends dangling free against the backs of his hands. He moved away from the partition. Shaking his arms, he could feel the rope slacken a bit, but the coils wouldn't move. They were wrapped too tightly over one another.

Rolling onto his back, he jackknifed his way back to the wagon. Alice sat on the floor, staring at him. Looking back over his own forehead, he could see her huge eyes, like those of a blind woman, glassy and motionless. Slocum crawled almost into her lap, then rolled on his stomach to show her the severed rope. She mumbled something as he sat up and leaned back against her. She turned her own back and groped for the loose ends. She found one and pulled on it. He could feel it fall away, and then Alice shifted her grip to the other end. Again she pulled, and again a coil came away.

Slowly, one by one, she tugged the coils loose until he could shake free of the last few. His wrists ached and his hands were numb. He saw the bloody fingers and the heels rubbed raw, but there was no time to waste. Leaning forward, Slocum untied his ankles. He stood on his own for the first time in hours, and thought he was going to fall over. His feet were numb, and the tingling sensation of his feet and ankles was maddening.

Rubbing his wrists to restore circulation, he knelt beside Alice and untied her hands. While she worked on the knots binding her ankles, he loosened the gag, clamping a hand over her mouth as the cloth came free.

He leaned closer to whisper. "We're not out of this yet."

She nodded that she understood.

"What are we going to do?" she whispered.

"I don't know. But whatever happens, you stay out of sight." Slocum tugged her to her feet and she hobbled along after him. He tried the ladder to the loft. It seemed sturdy enough, and he handed her up. "Go all the way up and stay there," he hissed.

"But . . ."

"Never mind, do as I say."

He watched her disappear over the lip of the loft, then dashed back to the corner. The tools were his only weapons. He found a pitchfork missing two tines, the rest rusty and brittle-looking. Slocum grabbed it and the hoe, then moved back toward the door.

He could hear voices approaching as he reached the wall. Flattening himself against the raw timber, he leaned the hoe against a stud, and hefted the pitchfork. The door hinges creaked, then stopped. Early sunlight spilled blood on the floor of the barn as Slocum drew a breath and held it.

"Now, Roy, remember what I told you," he heard McDonald say. "I don't want anything to happen to either one of them until I know what the hell happened to that money. Liz says he knows where it is, and I believe her."

"Don't worry about it, Mr. McDonald."

"I don't. But you should, Roy. I lose that money, and you'll work for me 'til hell freezes over to pay it back. You understand?"

"Yes, sir."

"Alright, then. You know where I'll be. If they tell you anything, you check it out. You find the money, then you can do whatever you want with Slocum."

"What about the girl?"

McDonald must have gestured, because Roy laughed. Footsteps receded and then the door swung wider. Roy's shadow splashed across the blood-red floor.

Slocum tried to disappear into the wooden wall. Roy, whistling through his teeth, stepped in and pulled the door shut behind him with a squeal of the hinges. It reminded Slocum of a stuck pig.

Shuffling across the dirt floor, Roy had his hands stuffed in his pockets. When he rounded the end of the wagon, Slocum started to move in behind him.

"Hey, sweetheart," Roy said, "where the hell are you?" He seemed baffled for a moment as Slocum tiptoed closer, then he turned as Slocum slipped on the dirt floor. His mouth flew open and he backed away a step. His hand was moving, almost as an afterthought, toward the gun on his hip. Slocum scrambled forward, the pitchfork in one hand, the other hand skittering along the ground as he tried to regain his balance.

Roy's fingers curled around the butt of the pistol and Slocum rose upward, extending the pitchfork at the same instant. Roy took another step back as his gun cleared the holster. And Slocum launched himself through the air. With no real base under him, the arc was feeble, but the pitchfork reached out and grazed Roy's gunhand, knocking the gun loose.

It landed right at his feet, and Slocum rolled to one side, bringing the rusty fork up at the same time. Roy bent to retrieve the pistol, his mouth flapping soundlessly. He was trying to shout, but he was either too surprised or too frightened. A guttural croak stuck in his throat as he grabbed the gun again.

Slocum stabbed at him with the fork, but Roy backed away again, losing his own footing in his haste. But he had the gun. Slocum got to his knees and brought the pitchfork back like a spear as Roy swung the muzzle around. Slocum let fly and the fork slammed into Roy just below the chest. The thud of metal on bone sounded strangely innocent in the darkened barn. Roy grunted as the wind was knocked out of him, and he dropped the gun to close both hands around the handle of the pitchfork.

He tried to pull it free as the bloody bubble burst through his lips, leaving a dark smear on his chin. He fell backward, through the band of light from the loft door, and lay there a moment, his legs twitching and his boot heels rapping on the hard-packed dirt. Slocum noticed his own Colt tucked in Roy's belt.

Roy's head and shoulders lay in the slice of sunlight, the rest of him in the shadows. Another ruby globe expanded between his lips, a smaller one inside it like a pair of fancy soap bubbles. They caught the sunlight and shimmered for a moment, then burst.

And Roy lay still.

Slocum got to his knees, panting like a wounded animal. Bending over the dead man, he snatched his pistol away. He looked up at the loft and saw Alice staring down at him out of the gray shadows. Her mouth was open and she shook her head. Then, as if it were the last act of some bizarre play, she pulled the tattered ruins of her dress up around her breasts and turned away.

20

Slocum stepped to the ladder and climbed up two rungs at a time. Alice backed out of the way as he hurled himself over the top. Through the open loft door, he watched as McDonald and a second man rode out through a split rail fence and vanished into the trees.

He felt Alice at his shoulder. "What's happening?" she asked.

"I don't know. Your boss is leaving, but that's all I can see. There's a small house, and a handful of horses. It's a good bet we're not alone."

"What are we going to do?"

"You're going to stay here. I'm going to borrow Roy's Peacemaker and see if I can't get us a couple of horses."

"What good will that do?"

"I don't know, maybe no good. But we can't just stay here."

"I'm frightened, Slocum. I . . ."

"Alice, we can't just roll over and die. You've been doing that so long, it's become a habit. But I can't do things that way. Especially not for scum like McDonald. Now you wait here. I'll be back as soon as I can."

"What if something happens to you? What'll I do?"

"You'll be no worse off than you were a half hour ago. And me, I'll be past worrying about it." He backed away from the open door and walked to the ladder. Hurrying down, he found Roy's pistol and stuck it in his belt.

Rather than use the front door, he forced open a window on the side of the barn away from the house and tumbled through it. He sprinted to the corner, ignoring the pain in his game leg, and watched the house for a few minutes.

Four horses shuffled nervously in the corral. They could just take the horses and make a run for it, but he wasn't sure that was a good gamble. He had no idea whether Alice could sit a horse, let alone ride one. And if they were followed, they'd be dead ducks. It made more sense to take McDonald's men head on and hope for the best. At least he wouldn't have to worry about getting shot in the back.

The sun was behind him, and it smeared red light on the dirty windows of the house. It was impossible to see through the glass, but he had to assume at least four men were inside. Roy and Cal had come in the wagon, so there could be as many as five or six.

And there was only one way to find out.

Slocum took several deep breaths, then dashed the thirty yards to the side wall of the house. He listened at the window, but the house was completely silent. Moving around to the rear of the cedar-shingled rancher, he found an open window. He still heard nothing but peered in under the raised sash.

It was dark inside, and he couldn't see anything clearly. The room appeared to be unused. Directly across from the window, he could just make out a tall rectangle etched in the wood with light. It took him a few seconds to realize it was a door in the far wall. Slocum grabbed the sash with both hands and raised it six inches, pressing on the wood to control its movement and dampening the rasp of wood on wood with the pressure.

It was open far enough to admit him, and Slocum leaned in through the window and pulled himself all the way inside, letting his feet hit the floor with a soft thud. He held his breath as he crouched just to the left of the opening, his eyes fixed on the bright outline ten feet away. It rippled for a few seconds, and Slocum tensed, thinking someone was about to open the door. He heard footsteps approaching, and the shadow blocked the light for what seemed like an eternity before the tread moved on past and the light returned.

Getting up on tiptoe, Slocum drew close to the doorway, pulling Roy's Colt from his pants and pointing it vaguely toward the center of the door panel. He'd already made up his mind to shoot at the first sign of movement. But no one came.

Slocum leaned against the doorframe, his ear pressed to the crack of light. He could hear soft voices on the far side, but the words were garbled. There were at least two men, but he couldn't tell how many more. The voices sounded so much alike it could have been a solitary lunatic talking to himself or an army of men sharing a single voice.

He put his hand on the knob, careful not to rattle it, and gave it a tentative twist. It moved easily and without a sound. Dropping to one knee, he looked through the crack right alongside the latch and saw that it had disengaged. Slocum pulled the door toward him, and it moved, but not without protest. Getting to his feet, he leaned into the panel with his shoulder while pulling the door toward him. It opened just far enough to clear the frame, but the angle of the door edge had closed the gap. He could no longer see any light from the far side.

Tugging the door open farther, he could see into the right side of the room beyond. Three men sat at a table, a tall, scorched coffeepot on a wooden block in front of them. Slocum wanted to barge in on them, but had to know whether they were the only ones in the house. Conscious that McDonald was widening his lead with every passing minute, Slocum cursed under his breath. "Come on, you bastards," he whispered. But they continued their chatter without any sense whatever of his urgency.

Growing more impatient by the second, he started counting. By the time he reached twenty he'd decided to open the door at one hundred, regardless of what happened. At seventy-three, one of the men scraped his chair back and stood up. He passed out of sight to the left, and Slocum could hear him talking to someone. Neither man at the table answered, and Slocum knew there was at least one more man in the house.

He stopped counting, waiting again to see what would happen. A moment later, the first man returned and resumed his seat. "You guys want some coffee?" he shouted.

And two men answered. So, Slocum thought, that makes five.

Surprise was now his only ally, and with six shells in the pistol and five targets, it was almost a standoff. He had his own gun, too, but you could only pull one trigger at a time, regardless of what the penny dreadfuls thought. Whether the men would see it that way was another matter. He knew that one man can handle several as long as none of them is willing to die. No one wants to be the first, and no one is ever sure that his friends will join him if he makes a move.

Slocum had seen it time and time again. Some drunken lout in a bar would cow the whole place, each of his terrorized victims alone in his own sweat. He understood the dynamics, but never ceased to wonder that it worked. Now, nervously shifting his grip on the butt of the captured Colt, he crossed his fingers and hoped that it would work just one more time.

He eased to the left, reaching across his body with his left hand to grab the doorknob. He jerked the door open and stood in the doorway, waving the pistol. One of the men at the table saw him immediately. His startled reaction caused the other two to turn.

"What the . . ." but Slocum held a finger to his lips. The man swallowed the rest of his words and raised his hands.

Softly, Slocum whispered. "Gents, lose your guns. Quietly. One at a time."

The men looked at one another, trying to decide who should go first. Ony one man was looking in his direction, and Slocum pointed with his chin. The man eased his pistol from its holster and set it on the table, then raised his hands. His two partners followed suit, and Slocum waved them up. When they were on their feet, he waved again, this time toward the right-hand wall. They moved quickly, almost eagerly, away from the temptation lying on the table in front of them.

Slocum kept an eye on the three men and stepped through the door. To the left, a half open door led into a second room. Slocum stepped to the table and tucked the three revolvers into his belt. "How many?" he asked, shaping the words, but not sounding them out.

Two men held up two fingers, and the third held up one. Slocum smiled. He gestured for the three men to enter the room he had just left, then followed them in. As the last of the three crossed the threshold, Slocum slammed the Peacemaker into the base of his skull, knocking him to his knees. The other two turned, but Slocum held a cautionary finger up. Stepping close, he lashed out with the pistol a second time, catching the nearer man under the chin with the muzzle. The man's head jerked back, and his companion caught him as he stumbled backward.

"Set him down," Slocum whispered. "Quietly. I don't want to have to shoot, but I will if you make me."

The third man lowered his unconscious partner to the floor, then held both hands out toward Slocum as if to say, "Take it easy, man."

Slocum glanced back through the open door, then backed into the room. He waved the third man through after him, then slipped behind him, pressing the pistol barrel up under his right ear. Slocum leaned close and hissed into the same ear, "Now, I want you to call the others, *all* of them. Don't be stupid, because that would be a mistake, and I won't give you a chance to make another. Understand?"

The man swallowed hard, then nodded. Slocum turned his prisoner, keeping the man's body between him and the half-open door. "Alright, go ahead," he whispered.

The man tried to call, but his voice wouldn't cooperate. It was a strangled croak. His throat was dry, and he was terrified. Slocum screwed the muzzle even harder into the bone just beneath the ear. "Go *on*, call them."

"Ray, come're a minute, will you?"

"What?" Slocum recognized the voice from the next room.

"Come're a minute, will ya? Bring Randy."

"What's the matter?"

"Nothing. Just come're, alright?"

"Yeah, yeah, yeah . . ." Ray was grumbling as he approached the doorway. He stepped through a moment later, followed by a man the same height but nearly twice the width and weight. "What's the . . ." He shook his head when he saw Slocum. "Damn!"

The big man behind him started to back away, but Slocum stopped him with a warning. "I wouldn't."

"What the hell do you *want*?" Ray snapped.

"Anybody else here?"

"Nope."

"If you're lying, I'll get you first."

"There's nobody here, dammit."

"Good. Sit down. Over here at the table, where I can watch you. Keep your hands flat on the table, both of you."

Slocum watched intently as they moved to the table and dropped into their chairs. When their hands were in place, he said, "I'm going to ask a few questions. I want answers, and I don't have the time or the inclination to fool around. So you better tell me what I want to know, and be quick. Where's McDonald going?"

The two men looked at one another.

"Denver," Ray said at the same time the big man was saying "Cheyenne."

Slocum cocked the Peacemaker. "Tell him, Ray, damn it," the third man croaked. Slocum could feel the prominent Adam's apple against his forearm bob up and down as the man swallowed hard.

Ray shook his head. "Alright, alright. He's going to Sterling."

"That's better. Where's Liz Holcom?"

"Denver."

"Where?"

"I don't know. Probably at the railyard. McDonald's taking his private train from Sterling. Just ahead of the first run."

"First run?"

"Yeah. The line's opening from Sterling to Denver this afternoon. Big ceremony in Denver. Sterling's the halfway point between Denver and Cheyenne."

Slocum leaned in to hiss in the third man's ear. "That right, partner?"

The man nodded, swallowing hard again. Slocum pushed him toward the far wall, keeping the pistol flush up against his neck. "Take that rope over there and tie them up. Be quick about it."

He backed away, waiting impatiently while the frightened cowhand tied Ray and the big man to their chairs. When he was finished, Slocum herded him into the next room, where he instructed him to tie the two men on the floor as well.

"Okay," Slocum said. "Now, give me your clothes."

"What?"

"Your clothes. Schuck 'em, boots too." When the man had stripped to his underwear, Slocum used the last of the rope to tie him hand and foot. Gathering the boots and clothes into a loose bundle, he ran for the barn.

He threw the door open. "Alice, come on, hurry." She ran toward him, still holding her dress together as best she could. "Can you ride a horse?" he asked.

She nodded. Handing her the bundle of clothes, he said, "Here, put these on."

21

Slocum skidded into the terminal just as the engine, belching black smoke from its huge stack, coughed out onto the main line and started to pull away. It towed a single car, and Slocum knew McDonald was aboard. Glancing over his shoulder, he saw Alice, wearing the stolen clothes, a good hundred yards behind.

As he saw it, Slocum had a choice. He could try to board the train, risking a gunfight with McDonald and his men, but he'd run the risk of killing the only man who knew for sure where Liz, Barbara, and the others were being held. If he backed off, the pressure of time was that much greater, but he knew he had an ace in the hole. McDonald didn't know where his money was. Until Liz cracked, he wouldn't harm her. That left the other three women in danger, and Slocum knew he might use them to force Liz to confess. If she gave in, all bets were off.

He heard a horn and jerked his head around in time to see a puff of steam rise up from behind the terminal. The flap of cloth caught his attention, and only then did he realize some sort of ceremony was under way. Red, white, and blue bunting snapped in the hot wind, suspended across the tracks on slender ropes.

Slocum spotted a man in grease-stained coveralls lumbering toward him.

"Hurry the hell up, cowboy," the man barked. "You want to ride, hop to it. You don't, then get the hell out of the way."

Slocum looked back toward the terminal as Alice rode up.

"What's going on?" he asked the man in coveralls.

"Maiden voyage, cowboy. Don't you read the papers?"

"No. What are you talking about?"

"First run. The Sterling line's carrying its first passengers today."

"I thought the line wasn't completed."

"It ain't, but that don't stop the boss. Hell, he'd run the bugger without any rails at all if he thought he could get away with it."

Slocum glanced at Alice, who seemed bewildered by the entire conversation. He started to say something but the trainman interrupted. "You want to ride, you better get movin'."

Slocum hopped down from the horse and handed the reins to Alice. He fished the key out of his pants and stuffed it into her palm. "Get to the room at the hotel, Alice. Stay there. I'll be back."

"Where are you going?"

He looked at the trainman, who answered his unspoken question. "Denver..."

Without waiting for her answer, he sprinted for the train, already starting to puff its way out of the station. He jumped and caught a handrail, swinging himself up onto the last boarding steps as the train rolled slowly by.

He rolled the heavy door aside and stepped into the car. Most of the seats were occupied. Farmers in their Sunday best sat with their families, while cowboys, already half drunk with anticipation, sipped whiskey from pint bottles and shouted to one another. The atmosphere was more like a party than a train ride. Slocum threaded his way down the aisle, sidestepping carpetbags and wicker baskets piled on the floor.

Halfway through the car, an empty double seat caught his eye, and he dropped into it with a sigh. He watched the conductor work his way to the rear, shouting "Tickets, please," as he tottered from side to side, balancing himself in countersway to the rocking of the car.

Slocum fished a pair of silver dollars out of his pocket and held them in his hand, nervously turning them over and over, like a rookie magician waiting for a summons to the stage. The heavy discs clanked loudly in his palm, but the heft of them seemed to calm him somehow. Slocum tried to shut out the ruckus and concentrate on what his next move should be. It was a comfort that McDonald wasn't that far ahead of him, but he was a long way from having the situation figured out.

Three seats ahead, the conductor leaned over to say something to a man sitting against the window. "May I have your ticket, sir?" he asked.

The cowboy to whom the question had been directed ignored him. He crouched against the window, his hat brim crushed up against the glass. Thinking perhaps the cowboy was asleep, the conductor tapped him on the shoulder. But, without moving his head, the cowboy snatched at the hand, grabbed the conductor's wrist, and pushed it away.

"I have to have your ticket," the conductor insisted, struggling to pull his arm free.

"I don't have one."

"Then you'll have to buy one, sir." The conductor stood erect, one hand on a hip, the other fiddling nervously in his pocket.

The cowboy shook his head. The man next to him leaned close and whispered something. Again the cowboy shook his head. "Mind your own business, Cal," he snapped. "I don't need no ticket."

At the sound of the name, Slocum's ears pricked up. He sat forward in his seat, trying to get a glimpse of either man. The man addressed as Cal calmed the conductor down, pulling him close and whispering something that seemed to satisfy him, if not mollify him. Slocum was unable to see the man's face, but he was fairly certain he'd recognized the voice.

The conductor continued on his rounds, taking Slocum's two dollars and returning him change Slocum didn't bother to count. When the ticket was inserted into the back of his seat, Slocum slid down, tipping his hat forward over his eyes and leaning against the side of the car. The trip was anything but smooth, but his hat cushioned the worst of the blows as his head bounced intermittently off the glass.

The racket around him seemed to grow louder as the raucous ranch hands emptied their whiskey and generally

behaved as if they were in a Saturday night saloon. Somebody sat next to Slocum, but he ignored the pressure on the
bench seat. Getting into a conversation would only distract
him and force him to tilt his hat back, at least enough to be
polite. At the moment, there were more important matters
to attend to.

Slocum was able to watch the man named Cal with one
eye, peering between his hat and the side of the car, but the
man sat quietly, ignoring the racket and saying nothing to
his irascible seatmate. Slocum checked his pocket watch,
then realized he didn't even know when they were sched-
uled to arrive in Denver. At the current rate of speed, it
would have to take at least four or five more hours. The
clacking of the wheels on the unsettled rails was more irri-
tating than restful, and the steady rapping of iron on iron
reminded him of nothing so much as a clock, ticking away
precious minutes.

Somewhere ahead, Kevin McDonald was on his way to
Denver and, presumably, to deal with Liz Holcom in a
manner Slocum could only guess at. What had moved him
to leave the barn without bothering to question Slocum a
second time? The only possibility that suggested itself to
him was that McDonald had learned something from another source, something that made questioning Slocum a
luxury. That did not bode well for Liz, or for Barbara either.

And just where did Barbara McDonough fit into the
picture? he wondered. She was anything but the innocent
child Liz Holcom had implied. That made him wonder
whether Liz had any idea who and what Barbara really
was. But then, he realized, he himself had no idea either.
A shrinking violet, she certainly wasn't. Nor was she a
babe in the woods. On the contrary, she seemed more sure
of herself than Liz. It was interesting, to say the least, and
more mysterious than Slocum wanted to believe. But then,
since the first moment he'd gotten involved with these
women, very little had been anything close to what it appeared to be.

The train slowed periodically, to bask in the applause of
small knots of people who gathered at strategic points

along the route to cheer. The railroad was still a novelty to many of them, and they recognized the role it would play in their future lives. Slocum growled impatiently to himself every time the train slowed, and every time the engineer yanked on the cord to sound his whistle. The piercing shriek seemed to cut right through him, reminding him that time was slipping away and that he had no control over it.

When it slowed for what seemed like the fiftieth time, he checked his watch again. The conductor stood in the back of the car, shouting unintelligibly, but the cheer that went up inside the car told Slocum they must be entering Denver. He shifted restlessly in his seat, watching Cal and his companion talking quietly under the uproar.

Cal stood and looked to the rear of the car. Slocum ducked his head behind his hat, but not before he'd seen what he needed to see. It was the same Cal, no question. He had his connection, even if McDonald was long gone. Stay on his tail, Slocum told himself, and you will find what you are looking for.

Buildings started to slip by, and they were far more substantial than anything Slocum had seen in weeks. Denver was to Sterling what Sterling was to a mud hut in the middle of nowhere. People lined the tracks on both sides of the train, forcing the engineer to back off on the throttle until the engine barely crept along. The shuddering of the floorboards was louder than the rumble of the big engine, and both were all but drowned by the incessant cheering that filled the car.

Cal stepped out of his seat, pushing his way toward the rear of the car. His sidekick was right behind him. Slocum permitted himself a sideways glance at the second man, but failed to recognize him. When they were safely past, Slocum tilted his hat back and turned to look out the window across the aisle to his left.

Out of the corner of his eyes, he could see Cal standing in the doorway, talking to the conductor. The big kid seemed like a good enough fellow, and Slocum found himself wondering how he had gotten mixed up with a bastard like McDonald. But then, he told himself, if he worried about that sort of thing, he'd spend all his time trying to explain a question that baffled ministers and philosophers alike. You have to deal with what is, he reminded himself.

The train finally lurched to a standstill, and the passengers began to file out. Slocum stood up quickly, slipping in among the knotted friends and clustered families, reaching the rear door in time to see Cal step into the train station. Slocum jumped down just as Cal reappeared. Glancing around the crowd, Slocum saw Cal's companion waiting impatiently at the far corner of the station. When Cal joined him, both men moved toward the front of the train, zigzagging to avoid the heavy crush of celebrating Denverites pressing up against the cars and shaking hands with passengers hanging from the open windows.

When he reached the engine, Slocum saw a swatch of blue-and-white cloth flapping just past the edge of the stack and he moved to the right. A makeshift platform had been built across the tracks. It was decked in bunting, and a throng milled around its base. Several men chatted among themselves atop the platform. Three of them, dressed in top hats and coats despite the heat, seemed impressed with the turnout and not a little with themselves.

Obviously, some sort of ceremony had been arranged to celebrate the first run from Sterling. And that could only mean one thing. Somewhere in the immediate vicinity, Kevin McDonald must be preparing to take his place on the platform. All Slocum had to do was to stand back and wait.

The pushing and shoving annoyed him, but Slocum allowed the crowd to flow around him like water around a stone, and he worked his way over toward the end of the terminal. With the building between him and the milling throng, he watched as Cal looked nervously around, as if he were expecting someone. Cal's companion leaned against the end of the platform, rolling a cigarette with intense concentration on the paper and tobacco in his hands.

A bugle sounded, and one of the top hats stepped to the front edge of the platform. He held his hands high in the air while the bugler finished an off-key rendition of "Reveille."

The crowd quieted slowly, and the bugler was forced to negotiate another chorus while everyone else was forced to endure listening to it. Finally, as if to save their ears from further assault, everyone shut up, seemingly at once.

The top hat lowered his hands. "Friends," he said, shouting to be heard at the back of the crowd. "This is a great day for Colorado." The crowd cheered lustily, and he was forced to wait before he could be heard again. "It's a great day for Denver..." Another cheer, this one not as long or as loud, "...and it's a great day, most especially, for Sterling."

The cheering broke out again, this time accompanied by a rhythmic clapping of hands. "And all of us, Colorado, Denver, and, again most especially, Sterling, owe a great debt to the man who made this afternoon possible." He held his hand out toward the small knot behind him on the platform. "And I'm sure we haven't heard the last of this great Coloradan. I'm sure there is greatness in his future, and his greatness is in yours..." He raised his voice now, shouting at the top of his lungs in anticipation of the coming tumult. "...Kevin Alexander McDonald."

Slocum watched quietly as McDonald stepped to the front of the platform with his own hands raised high above his head. "And you haven't heard the last of me, either, Mr. McDonald," Slocum whispered.

22

Slocum leaned against the wall, the rented horse jerking at the reins with nervous tosses of his head. McDonald was still inside, and the sun was already down. If McDonald didn't make a move soon, Slocum might have to force his hand. He had hoped to avoid a confrontation until he knew where Liz was being held. The women were McDonald's trump card, and Slocum had to massage the odds, to make sure the game was over before he got a chance to play it out.

Cal and the other man were inside, drowsing in chairs against one wall of the office. Lamp light bathed the alley, and Slocum stood in the shadows, watching silhouettes glide across the ground as McDonald and another man moved restlessly around the large desk. They seemed to be arguing, but neither man raised his voice. In outline on the sandy ground, the sharp hand gestures and waving arms looked like bad shadow animals made by a well-meaning but inept uncle.

Slocum was running out of patience. Twice, he resolved to force the odds and charge into the office with his gun drawn, but each time he managed to control himself. There was no doubt in his mind that McDonald would lead him to Liz. The question was, when?

Crossing the alley, he dropped below the window ledge and tried to listen to the animated conversation, but the closed window allowed only meaningless scraps out into the night. Then he heard a door bang, and he took off his hat to get closer. Peering cautiously through a lower corner of the clean glass, he saw McDonald already through a door opposite the window. Cal and the other man from the train slipped past him, and McDonald pulled the door shut with a loud slam. The glass in front of Slocum's nose rattled in its frame.

Slocum recrossed the alley and climbed onto his horse, nudging it down the alley toward the back of the building. A moment later, a rear door opened and Cal came out. McDonald stood there, a black shadow backlit by orange, and waved his hands. "Now you wait until I get there, Cal. You understand me?"

"Yes, sir, I do," Cal said.

"I'll be there as soon as I can get rid of this buffoon."

"Anything you want me to tell Ronny?"

"No. I'll handle that. As soon as I find out where the money is, I want you and Ronny to go back to Sterling. I want that cowboy out of the way. But not yet . . ."

Cal mounted a coal-black mare, all but invisible in the shadows, and waited for his companion. When the second man untied his own horse and climbed into the saddle with a squeak of leather, McDonald said, "Pete, I want you to do exactly what Cal tells you. No mistakes, no arguments, no bullshit. He knows what I want. He tells you something, you do it. Am I making myself clear?"

Pete grunted. "This is your last chance, Pete. I have taken all I'm going to from you."

"Yeah, yeah, I know."

McDonald slammed the door and disappeared. "Let's go," Cal said.

Slocum waited in the darkness until Cal and Pete rode past. He let them get a slight lead, then fell in behind them. Following them at night was worse than balancing on the edge of a knife. Close enough to see them, he might betray his presence. Far enough back to be safe, he might lose them.

They had gone just over a mile when they hit a railroad spur. Cal and Pete settled into a steady lope, following the tracks. Slocum fell back a little, hoping the spur would lead him where he wanted to go. Another mile and Slocum spotted a light burning far ahead. It glinted off the rails but he couldn't see anything beyond the orange point and its dim reflection on the polished metal of the tracks.

He could no longer see either rider now, but he could hear their horses on the rocky soil. As the glow drew closer, gliding toward him like a running light on a ship, a point in the heart of darkness, he could sense, rather than see, the presence of something there. He fought the urge to charge headlong through the night, knowing that he was getting close to his goal, close to getting McDonald out of his life altogether. *If* he was careful, and *if* he didn't let his impatience work against him.

Another quarter mile and Slocum saw the outline of a large building, longer than a barn and not as tall. It seemed to stretch across the tracks, but he couldn't see it clearly enough to be certain. He reined in and could no longer hear the horses ahead of him. Slocum slid out of the saddle and tugged his horse into a clump of pines. Walking another hundred yards, he reached a point where he could see either end of the huge building.

Slocum lay down next to the tracks and sighted along the nearer rail. It led right to the center of the building, but it wasn't possible to see where it went after that, if anywhere. Drifting away from the rails, he slipped in among the trees and headed toward the building's left corner. The closer he got, the larger the building seemed. A single lantern hung over a pair of broad slatted doors. The front wall was windowless, a massive black barrier directly across the tracks. Then Slocum realized it must be some sort of storage or maintenance barn for the rolling stock.

He crept closer to the corner, approaching it at an angle with one ear cocked for the slightest noise. He held his breath until his fingers came into contact with the rough wood of the wall. Slipping down along the side, he found it, too, to be windowless. A single door at the back corner was locked, and he moved around to the rear. Another pair of doors, as large as those at the front, occupied the center, and the tracks swept away to the north, as shiny and straight as those on the opposite side.

But this side had windows. A single row set high on the wall ran from one corner to the other. They were far out of his reach and there was no way he could boost himself up to look inside. Slocum tiptoed across the back wall to the other end. He waited there a moment, listening. So far, he had heard nothing. And he had seen no sign that anyone was inside. He was sure he would have heard the massive doors open if Cal and Pete had taken their mounts inside.

Peering around the corner of the building, he spotted a half dozen horses, hitched to a long rail bolted into the side of the building. Slocum bit his lower lip. Six meant at least six men. The odds were lousy and getting lousier. McDonald would be along in an hour or less, making them even worse.

On the far side of the horses, a wooden ladder ran up to the roof. Like the hitching rail, it seemed to be bolted into the wall of the building, and beyond the ladder he could see what appeared to be the frame of a small door. Easing past the horses, patting their flanks to keep them quiet, he darted in against the wall again. At the door, he pressed his ear to the splintery wood for a moment. He could hear nothing inside. Behind him, the horses snorted uneasily. He tried the door, and it moved easily, on well-oiled hinges, but he didn't want to use it if he didn't have to.

Tiptoeing back to the horses, he slid in beside Cal's mare and found a Remington carbine in the boot. He checked the magazine, found that it was fully loaded, then rummaged through the saddlebags until he found a box of shells. He stuffed the half-empty box into his pocket, then collected the remaining weapons from the other horses. He knew what he was going to do now, and he needed every edge.

Carting the rifles and carbines off into the trees, he lay them against the base of a tree and kicked leaves and pine needles over them. It wasn't a perfect cover, but in the dark, they might well have been thrown in the river. He sprinted back to the barn and started up the ladder, moving cautiously from rung to rung, testing each to make sure it would hold his weight. The wood was new, and the whole contraption securely mounted.

As he reached the roofline, Slocum stopped to take stock. Covered in split shakes, the roof offered secure footing, but it would be difficult to walk across it without making a sound. Boosting himself up and over, he sat down carefully, taking his boots off and laying them on their sides. He stood in his stockinged feet and examined the roof. Slanting away at a gentle angle from a point roughly at its center, two broad planes, each broken by several flat windows, stretched to the far end of the building. The skylights glowed dully with light from the interior of the barn.

Slocum walked gingerly toward the nearest skylight. Standing there, high above the glass, it was like looking down into another world. Everything below was orange and shadow. A huge mosaic of rails occupied the center of the floor, and off to each side, several pairs of rails, some empty, some bearing railroad cars, stretched toward either side wall.

Slocum dropped to his stomach and leaned out over the dusty glass. He saw no sign of life. The lights burned as if they were on forever, but nothing moved. Two of the cars on the opposite side of the barn, fancier than most but still recognizable as passenger cars, were lit from inside. Slocum wanted to get a better look and scurried across the roof to a point just above them and to their right side.

He could see through the windows of the nearer car, but its body blocked the windows of the one more distant. The cars were nearly thirty feet below him, and the acute angle between skylight and car window didn't permit him to see much. At one end, he spotted two moving shadows on the floor of the car. At the other end, more shadows spilled on the rails through a pair of windows. It was impossible to tell whether they were cast by the same two people. And the blurred edges of the silhouettes concealed everything, including the sex, of their owners.

Moving up over the peak of the roof, Slocum knelt over another skylight. This time, he could see into the other car. A man he didn't recognize sat at a table, cleaning a pistol. Rags and a small vial of oil sat beside his hands on the table, and the revolver had been broken down. The man worked busily at the cylinder. Slocum almost admired the meticulous attention to detail. He guessed the man must have seen some army time to be so careful about his weapon. Either that or he was a man who depended on his gun more than most. And Slocum didn't care to think about the implications of that possibility.

Getting to his feet, Slocum tiptoed back to the far edge and sat down to put on his boots. Taking the ladder two rungs at a time, he was moving almost recklessly, goaded by the knowledge that McDonald was right behind him. And McDonald was certainly not coming alone.

Slocum tried the small door again and pulled it open just far enough to slip inside. He closed it softly and moved to the back wall of the barn. Using the dark, silent cars for cover, he reached the center doors and skipped over the tracks to duck down behind a massive engine, its great, bulbous stack towering above him like some bizarre rock formation.

He could see the front end of both lit cars from where he was, but the direct route was too exposed. Slocum opted to continue along the back wall into the corner. From there, he could just make out the rear ends of the cars. A big, boxy cattle car blocked his view of any of their windows.

Taking a deep breath, he snicked the safety off the borrowed Remington and levered a shell into the chamber. The noise of metal on metal sounded impossibly loud in the stillness. He pressed back against the wall, certain that someone had to have heard the noise. But everything remained as silent as it had been.

Slocum worked his way closer, listening for the first sound of movement in either of the cars. In a crouch directly behind the cattle car, he could see through the windows of the nearer car. Thick drapes framed each side window, but his view was unobstructed. He could see details of the luxurious appointments and the lamps suspended from the car's wooden ceiling. But nothing moved. As far as he could tell, the car was empty.

He sprinted across the gap, skipping over the rails and planting his feet between the ties. At the side of the car, directly under a window, he listened again. And again he heard nothing. On tiptoe, he raised himself as far as he could to peer inside. The far side of the car was occupied by long, velvet-covered divans. Curtains hung between them, bunched against the wall, dangling from overhead rods allowing them to close around each divan, cutting the car into separate chambers.

On one divan, in jeans and a blue shirt, lay Barbara McDonough. She seemed to be asleep. Slocum twisted his head to try to see more when Barbara stirred; as she rolled over, he saw that her hands were shackled together, the chain secured to a metal fixture bolted into the wall. Her eyes opened suddenly, and Slocum realized she was staring directly at him. He steeled himself for the scream he was certain would come.

Like a man in a dream, Slocum watched as Barbara's lips parted in slow motion. Her mouth opened slowly, and Slocum's nerves started to coil like springs. Then, even more slowly, she stuck out her tongue.

Then she winked.

23

Slocum signaled with his hands and Barbara directed him to the rear door with a quick nod of her head. On the rear platform, he listened for a moment, then pressed the door open with one hand. It swung quietly inward, bumping against a wooden door to some sort of closet. Slocum let the door close behind him, muffling the latch with his fingers, then peeked through a curtain into the car's interior.

Barbara still lay on the divan, her head back on the single cushion. Beyond her, another figure, a woman judging by the hair, lay on a second sofa. Slocum could not see her face, but there was no mistaking the hair. It was Liz Holcom.

Across a broad aisle, against the other side of the car, two men sat at a foldaway table, playing cards. There was no sign of Karen or Mabel. Slocum was disappointed. It would have been far easier if all the women had been together, but then McDonald would have thought of that. Slocum rubbed his free hand across his mouth and chin. In the silence, the rasp of skin on two-day-old whiskers sounded like a sawmill going full tilt.

What the hell am I going to do now? he wondered. One of the cardplayers jerked his head around, and for a moment Slocum was afraid he might have been talking aloud. The man stared at the window behind Barbara for a long moment, then turned back to his game. "This place gives me the creeps," he mumbled.

"You just can't handle a bad hand." His opponent laughed.

"Shut up and give me two . . ."

Slocum sighed with relief. For the moment, square one seemed like paradise. He had only one course of action. He didn't like it, but he didn't see how he could do anything else. He found a pair of pillows on a shelf over the door. He grabbed one, a thick bolster stuffed with what felt like goose down, and pressed it against the muzzle of the Remington. It was crude, but it would dampen the sound of a gunshoot.

Shaking his head, he nudged the drapes aside and stepped into the car. The light dimmed his vision for a moment, and he froze, the Remington pointed at the back of the nearer cardplayer. He took a step, gritting his teeth and praying to himself.

The cardplayer dropped a card, Slocum watched it slide like a kite with a broken string, then skid to the floor. It was the jack of hearts. The man bent to retrieve it, and Slocum found himself staring into the eyes of the second man, who seemed for a moment not to realize what was happening. Then, as if a surge of electricity had jolted him, he started to get up.

Slocum shook his head, patting the Remington and shaking a finger. The man froze, halfway out of his chair, his mouth open and fluttering like the wings of a moth.

Bending to retrieve the card, the first player must have sensed something. As his hand pinned the card to the floor, he turned his head toward Slocum. He, too, suddenly turned to stone.

Softly Slocum said, "That's right, gents, nice and easy. Nobody has to get hurt. It's up to you."

Instead of soothing the men, Slocum's words seemed to galvanize them. The first player fell out of his chair while the second kicked his own chair over backward. He made the mistake of reaching for his gun and Slocum fired. He aimed wide, catching the man in the ribs just above the belt. He spun to one side and sat down heavily. A cloud of feathers filled the air for a moment, then drifted to the floor.

The first man came to rest against Barbara's divan. He lay there stunned, his hands stretching out toward Slocum in surrender. "Alright," he said, "alright. Don't shoot me, man. Don't . . ."

"The keys . . ." Slocum snapped.

"Right here, man, right here. Don't shoot me, now. I'm just getting the keys." He brought one hand to his chest and fished around in his shirt pocket for a moment, then pulled out a pair of shiny keys on a short chain.

Nodding toward Barbara, Slocum said, "Give them to her."

The man lay flat on his back, arcing his hand up and over. Barbara's hand closed over the keys and Slocum stepped to the left, watching the man on the floor while drawing closer to the small table. He could hear the second man moaning, but he couldn't see anything other than his feet.

Barbara freed her hands, then rushed to unchain Liz, who was similarly shackled. It hit Slocum all at once that Liz hadn't moved. Not when he first spoke, and not even when the shot was fired. Barbara unlocked the chain and tugged Liz to an upright position. Slocum knelt to keep down below the window and crabwalked to the first card-player. He jerked the man's gun from its holster and tucked it in his belt.

Disarming the second man, he tugged him to a sitting position. The man was bleeding heavily, but the wound, although painful, wasn't serious.

"Close the drapes," Slocum hissed, and Barbara turned to look at him. "The drapes," he said again.

Realizing what he wanted, she pulled the cord and a thick blue cloth swept across the window. She let Liz fall back on the divan for a moment and closed the second drape.

He handed Barbara one of the pistols. "You might have to use this," he said.

She swallowed hard, but nodded. "I can do it. Don't worry about me."

"Where are the others?"

"In the other car."

"How many men?"

"I don't know. Three, maybe four."

"What's wrong with Liz?"

"I don't know. She's been like that since they brought me here this morning."

"You need help getting these two chained up?"

Barbara shook her head. "No. You'd be surprised what a little brutality can do to your perspective."

"Are you alright?"

"I am now . . ."

"You stay here. I don't care what happens. You stay inside."

She nodded. "I'm a big girl, Slocum."

It was his turn to nod. He walked toward the back door and paused. "Maybe you better close the drapes on this side, too. If they can't see you, you'll be safer."

He didn't wait to see whether she listened. Switching the Remington to his left hand, he dropped to the ground and moved in between the two cars. He listened under the nearest window, but there was no sign they'd heard anything.

This time, he felt more comfortable. With half the problem solved, he no longer had to worry about the sound of the gun. He'd felt a little silly holding the pillow, but it just might have saved all their lives.

He remembered the man inside cleaning his gun. Something told him this car was not going to be quite so easy. Standing on the rail, he managed to get a look into the car. He saw Karen immediately, sitting in a chair with her back to the window. He could see her reflection in the opposite glass. Like Liz, she had her eyes closed. Her breathing seemed so shallow he wondered for a second whether she was breathing at all.

Mabel was nowhere to be seen. He had wanted to know where she was before he made his move. If he could see her, he could prevent her being used as a hostage. But there was no time to waste. He'd have to take the risk.

He climbed onto the platform at the back end of the car. The door opened just as easily as that of the first car. He slipped inside and pushed the curtain aside with the muzzle of the Remington. Through the narrow gap, he could make out the man at the table, still working over a weapon. The pistol was back on his hip, and he had a Winchester carbine in pieces on the table. Beyond him, two more men dozed on one of the divans, their hats tilted forward and their legs crossed. He recognized Cal and Pete by their clothes.

Slocum pushed the curtain even farther and started to lean. The man at the table was so fast, Slocum wasn't even sure he had moved. The slug tore through the drapes just over his left shoulder. Without waiting for the man to move, Slocum fired once, jerked the Remington's lever and fired again. This time, the shots exploded in the confined space. The nearly silent spit of the muffled shot had been replaced by thunder.

The man started to rise, his right arm limp at his side, his gun on the floor where he had dropped it. Slocum fired again, this time into the ceiling, as the two sleeping cowboys, startled by the gunfire, jumped to their feet and went for their own guns at the same instant.

"Hold it!" Slocum barked. "Just hold it . . . Drop your damn guns." The cowboys pulled their guns with fingertips and dropped the pistols to the floor. Slocum watched with one eye, keeping the other on the wounded stranger.

The wounded man stared at him from the bottom of two black pools. Slocum had never seen eyes like them before. They were like two holes in the midnight sky, full of a darkness that had nothing to do with the heavens. He gripped his wounded bicep with the spread fingers of his left hand. His light green shirt was stained a bright red, and the blood trickled through his fingers and ran down the sleeve of the shirt in wriggling streams.

"You better kill me, cowboy," he said. "Because if you don't, I sure as hell will kill you. Now or later."

The voice was deep and resonant. Like the great pipes of a church organ, it seemed to swell and fill the tight space with its own echo. But the voice was as flat as the dead eyes, completely empty of emotion. The man spoke about the end of his own life with a perfect absence of passion.

Slocum swallowed hard. He wondered whether the man were putting up a good front, or if he meant what he said.

The debate was short-lived. Staring into those bottomless eyes, Slocum had no doubt at all. There was no way in hell he was going to kill an unarmed man, even one who asked for it. But there was also no doubt that the man would kill him at the first opportunity.

Slocum's eyes danced from the two cowboys to the black-eyed man and back.

"Who is he?" Slocum asked the two hands.

Both men shook their heads.

"Tie him up," Slocum said, trying to keep his own voice free of emotion.

The cowboys looked at one another as if he'd asked them to bite their own heads off. It was something so inconceivable to them, they seemed not to understand the command.

"Do it," Slocum said, jerking another round into the Remington. "Now!"

Pete, the taller of the two, shrugged, then looked around for something to tie the man with. His eyes settled on the thick drapery cord, and he tugged on one end until it came free.

"Stay clear," Slocum warned. "Don't get between him and me."

The cowboy nodded as if he understood. He approached gingerly, with the cord dangling from his hands. Reaching out cautiously, Pete waited for the man to place his wrists together in front of him, at belt level. He cleared his throat, then started to loop the cord around the motionless hands.

And a second later, Pete was on the floor. His legs kicked wildly and Slocum took his eyes away for a second. The stranger moved, and Slocum fired again. The shot went wide and the stranger dove to the floor, reaching for one of the discarded pistols. Slocum let go of the Remington and reached for his own Colt. He had it out as the stranger closed his hand around the butt of the nearest pistol. Slocum fired once, then again, and a third time. Each slug found its mark, and the stranger's body jumped with every hit.

Slocum could see the sudden puffs of cloth as each bullet struck, dimpling the man's shirt for an instant, the dim-

ple then turning bright red. Over and over, he could see it
in his mind's eye. The stranger lay still, but again and
again, Slocum saw the bullets strike, the dimpling cloth,
the spurt of bright red blood.

The smell of gunpowder was overwhelming. It cut
through the air and burned his nose and lungs. Slocum
looked at Cal, who had dropped to his knees beside Pete.
His hands were cupped on his knees as he bent over. The
handle of the knife in Pete's chest seemed to mesmerize
him. Three times, he started to reach for the ornate antler
handle, and three times he pulled his hand away, the way a
child pulls away from a fascinating flame as he feels the
heat.

"Jesus Christ, Petey. Jesus Christ, Petey. Jesus, Jesus,
Jesus." It started as a mumble and exploded into a heart-
rending wail. Cal turned on the stranger, already dead on
the floor, and started to pound him with both fists. Again
and again, he hammered at the dead man's back and
shoulders. "You killed my brother, you bastard. Bastard,
you bastard. You killed him."

Slocum walked toward the kid. He dropped to one knee
and put out a hand to touch the young man's shoulder.
"Come on, son, you can't hurt him no more."

The kid looked up at him with tears streaming down his
face. "My brother's dead," he whispered. "Deader'n hell."

"I know," Slocum said. "But . . ."

The horrible wail tore the night apart before Slocum
could finish.

"What the hell was that?" he shouted.

"Mr. McDonald's train," Cal said. "I got to open the
door."

24

"Alright, Cal, when I tell you, you just ease that door open like nothing's wrong."

Cal gulped. "Yes, sir," he said.

"And Cal?"

"Yeah?"

"One wrong move and you're a dead man."

Cal nodded. The kid reached up over his head for the latch holding the doors closed. Slocum leaned back against the wall, the Remington aimed at Cal's midsection. "Alright, go ahead."

The door rumbled as it moved to one side, sliding on greased rollers along the inside of the barn wall. The puffing of the engine grew louder as the opening widened. Finally, the door slammed into the stop and Cal moved quickly to the other one.

The inside of the barn was bathed in light from a large lantern on the front of the engine. Impatiently the engineer tugged on his whistle, and Cal jumped out of his skin.

Slocum tensed as the second door slid away. He was on a tightrope, and somebody was trying to shake him off. When the rails were clear, the engine squealed as its huge driver wheels started to turn. It rolled forward, the ground trembling with its weight. As it passed through the open doorway, the sound of it seemed to fill the huge barn and stretch its seams. Slocum fingered the Remington's trigger nervously. His palms were damp, and a trickle of sweat ran down between his shoulder blades.

Cal looked at him, expectantly, his hands half raised and hovering like hummingbirds just above his shoulders. Slocum jerked the barrel down, and Cal lowered his hands.

Stepping toward the kid, he said, "You can get on out of here, if you want to."

"Yes, sir, thank you, Mr. Slocum."

He was gone before his words even registered. The engine shut down. Its boiler pinged and popped as it began to cool. The engineer bled the pressure with a sudden explosive hiss, and then silence descended on the barn. The distant chiming of the slowly cooling metal faded still further and then was gone. Slocum stepped behind the single car and waited to see what would happen next.

The crunch of feet on sand caught his ear and he peered down along the left side of the short train. The engineer stood beside his engine, wiping his hands on a dirty rag. But where the hell was McDonald?

Slocum climbed onto the rear platform of the passenger car and pushed the door open. As he stepped inside, he saw McDonald just disappearing through the far door. He sprinted through the car and stepped into the dark vestibule. He could hear McDonald talking to someone outside, and he waited impatiently, trying to get a sense of the opposition. He heard three voices, one of which could have belonged to the engineer. Then McDonald shouted, "Cal? Where the hell are you? Hey, Cal . . . I need you here a minute. Come on, dammit."

Slocum stepped onto the front platform. He saw four men picking their way across the tracks toward the lighted cars. Cursing, Slocum jumped to the ground. The men heard the noise and turned toward him.

"Cal, that you?" McDonald shouted. He took a couple of steps back toward the engine, then, as if he sensed something was wrong, he stopped. "Cal?"

Slocum dropped into a crouch. "Cal's gone," he said.

"Who is that? Who's there?"

"It's me, Slocum."

"Slocum? What the . . ." McDonald backed up, tripping over a rail and landing heavily on the ground. "You sonofabitch . . ."

McDonald's three companions melted into the shadows. Slocum skipped to the left and lay flat, hugging the ground behind one of the rails. From his position, he could look down along the sides of both lighted cars. Since he couldn't see the four men, he concentrated his attention on the pools of light at each end of the cars.

"You bit off more than you can chew here, Slocum."

"You think so?"

"Give it up now and we can settle this quietly."

"Too late for that, McDonald. And don't count on any help from your boys, here. It's not in the cards."

A shadow suddenly leapt for the platform stairs of the left car and Slocum sighted and squeezed off a shot. The shadow pitched backward off the stairs and lay still. "That's one, gents," Slocum shouted. "You can leave, if you want. No sense getting yourself killed for scum like McDonald."

The words echoed back at him from the far corners of the barn. They faded away, leaving a silence even more profound.

"Slocum, you bastard, I want my money. All you have to do is tell me where it is, and you can walk away from this."

"And what about the women?"

"What about them?"

"Do they walk away, too?"

"Hell, I don't care. It's up to them."

"Is it really?"

"Women are a dime a dozen, Slocum. Hell, you know that."

"Then why didn't you let them go the first time?"

"I told you, the money. Nobody steals from me, Slocum. Nobody, you understand?"

Slocum didn't bother to answer. In the quiet, he could hear someone whispering. Slocum rolled to the right and lay still again, steeling himself for the next move. He didn't have long to wait. Footsteps thudded toward him, but he couldn't see anything. Aiming low, straight at the sound, he squeezed the trigger, then fired a second time. The footsteps stopped, but he had missed, and he knew it.

They were setting him, spreading out to try to catch him in a crossfire. Carefully, Slocum backed over the rail behind him. Trying not to make a sound, he moved so slowly it made his muscles ache. He glanced over his shoulder for an instant and was startled when McDonald shouted again.

"Slocum, what the hell are you doing this for? What's in it for you?"

Slocum didn't answer.

"Slocum, I'm talking to you, dammit. Answer me."

"Not on your life," Slocum whispered.

Squeezing his eyes to slits, he stared at the last place he had heard footsteps. His eyes caught the pale thin line of orange light where the lantern reflected off the polished surface of the rails. The line was almost perfect, except for one spot, where it was interrupted for a foot or so. Straining, he could see nothing beyond the rail, but something had to be there. Something was blocking the light. He lay the Remington down without a sound.

Drawing his Colt, he sighted it just above the break in the band of light. If he was right, it would be a reasonable trade off, giving away his position in exchange for reducing the odds. If he was wrong, it just might be the last mistake he got the chance to make. Holding his breath, he waited for some sign, some indication that he was on the money. When none came, he bit his lower lip.

Here goes nothing, he thought.

Slocum squeezed the trigger gently. The big Colt bucked and his concentration was so intent that its thunder startled him. He fired twice more, beginning to roll even as he fired the third shot. He hit the Remington and pushed it away with his right hand.

Sparks flew from the rail where he had been, but the shots had come from only two guns. He lay still as the sound of the guns died away. He heard a groan, and McDonald hissed, "Shut up, damn you."

"Forget it, McDonald. That's two down. Time's running out, man. You ready to give it up?"

"The hell with you." McDonald opened fire, emptying his gun in his rage. The remaining gunman started to run. Slocum tossed a slug at him as he reached the open door, but it sailed over his head and out into the night. Slocum waited patiently. He wasn't reckless enough to assume McDonald had only a single weapon. In the darkness, he could hear the sound of empty shells clattering on the rails, then the *snick—snick—snick* of a new load rammed home. The click of the cylinder as it locked slapped at the walls, then was swallowed by the night. The fleeing man had mounted up, and his horse galloped off into the darkness.

"It's you and me now, McDonald."

"Go to hell."

Slocum opened the Colt and slipped the three empties out, then reloaded. As he jammed the last cartridge home, McDonald bolted. He ran down between the two lighted cars, and Slocum lost sight of him. Getting to his feet, he charged across the barn. Reaching a spot between the two cars, he saw McDonald swing up and out of sight.

Slocum cursed and sprinted toward the front end of the car. Barbara and Liz were inside, and he still didn't trust Barbara to use the gun. She had been devastated by the last time. That had to make her uncertain, and McDonald wouldn't hesitate. Slocum leapt to the stairs of the front platform, his boots thumping on shiny metal. He shoved the door open and barged into the car.

Too late.

Barbara stood there facing the far door. The wounded man was unconscious, spread-eagled on a divan. His hands shackled to the wall. The other prisoner sat quietly, as if he were a spectator at a play. McDonald, his hands slightly elevated, still held his revolver. Slocum could not get a clear shot.

"Now, Babs . . . can I call you Babs?" McDonald oozed. "You know you're not going to shoot me. I know it and you do, too, isn't that right?"

Barbara didn't answer.

McDonald pressed his advantage. "Look, this is all some sort of giant misunderstanding. Slocum, there, doesn't give a damn about you. All he cares about is Liz and the money. My money. Money she *stole* from me. Is that the kind of man you can trust?"

Barbara started to turn, and Slocum shouted, "Don't take your eyes off him. He's just waiting for the chance."

"Shut up, Slocum," McDonald snapped. "She's a big

girl. She can think for herself. She doesn't need you to tell her what to do. Isn't that right, Babs? You can think for yourself, can't you?"

"Yes. I can think for myself, Mr. McDonald."

"It's Kevin. And listen, now, you can understand why I want my money back, can't you? I mean, I'm a businessman. I earned it, and it belongs to me."

"What's wrong with Liz?" Barbara asked. Her voice quavered and it was just above a whisper.

"What?"

"I asked you what was wrong with Liz, and the other girls."

"Nothing. Nothing at all."

"Then why are they like that?"

"Like what, Babs? I don't know what you're asking me." McDonald was pushing too hard. He was on the edge of losing it, and Slocum crossed his fingers.

Barbara shook her head. "Yes you do, you know perfectly well what I'm asking you. Why won't you answer me?"

"I don't. I swear, I . . ."

"Liar!"

"Now don't do that, Babs. Don't call me names. I don't like it."

"It's Barbara . . ."

"What?"

"Barbara, my name is Barbara, and I hate to be called Babs."

"Alright, fine. I understand that. I don't like it when people call me Kev. I can understand that. I can."

"Then answer my question, Kev. Now!"

"I already told you, there's nothing wrong. I just . . . well, I gave them a little something. Something to calm their nerves, you see. They were upset, and I could understand that, but . . ."

"What? What did you give them?"

"It's nothing, just a little medicine."

"What kind of medicine?"

"Nothing you've ever heard of."

"What was it?" Barbara cocked the pistol. "Answer me, dammit."

McDonald extended his arms, palms out, the pistol still in his right hand.

"Now, don't do that. Don't . . . Opium, alright, opium. Just to calm them down."

It was slipping away, and McDonald knew it. Slocum moved to the side, trying to get a clear shot, but the car was too narrow, and Barbara too close to McDonald. He saw McDonald's fingers close over the butt of the pistol.

As the hand started to come down, Slocum shouted, "Look out!"

He rushed forward as the gun went off. Barbara fell to the floor. McDonald stood there, teetering on his boot heels and staring at the hole in his chest. The gun fell from his fingers and he curled into a ball as he fell.

Barbara looked up at Slocum as he knelt beside her. "Why didn't you shoot?" she said. "I got out of the way. Why didn't you shoot?"

Slocum shook his head. "It all happened too fast."

She closed her eyes.

25

Slocum sat on the bed. Liz stood in front of him, her hands on her hips. "You got a lot of damn nerve, Slocum."

"It was just a suggestion."

"Thank you very much."

"Well, it makes sense to me. You said you had ten thousand. You offered to pay me a thousand. Now, if I remember my basic math, one from twenty-five is twenty-four. You keep your nine, which is all you would have had left anyway, if you had been telling the truth. That leaves fifteen. Cut four ways, that's thirty-seven fifty."

"Why four?" Liz was smiling in spite of herself.

"Karen, Mabel, Barbara, and Alice."

"Why Alice? She wasn't part of the original deal."

"That's true, she wasn't." Slocum grinned right back at her. "But if it hadn't been for Alice, I never would have found you. I think that entitles her to a share."

"You are one generous bastard, Slocum. When it comes to cutting up somebody else's money, anyway."

"Look, it's just a suggestion."

"What do you want to do, have them vote on it?" Liz laughed. "Oh, hell, you win. Do it!"

Slocum grinned even more broadly. "As a matter of fact, I knew you'd see it my way," he said. He reached under the bed and pulled out four moderate-sized canvas bags. He tossed them in turn to each of the four women, who sat on the floor behind Liz. To a woman, their mouths were agape.

"It's mostly paper," he said, "but the gold makes it a little heavy. I guess you all can handle it, alright, though."

The women chattered among themselves, and Liz walked over to Slocum and leaned forward to give him a kiss on the forehead. He reached under the bed and pulled out a larger bag and handed it to Liz. She nodded. "Thank you," she said.

"Don't mention it."

"You know, Slocum, if I didn't know better, I'd think you were some kind of knight in somewhat tarnished armor."

Slocum rested a hand on her hips. "I like you, too, Liz."

"I guess I better get going," she said.

"What are you going to do?" he asked.

"I don't know. I think California might be nice. Maybe I'll open a boarding house." She laughed. "If things get rough, it's easy to convert." She winked, and Slocum squeezed her hip.

"Good luck."

Barbara got to her feet. "I think we all owe Slocum a vote of thanks," she said.

The others nodded and tripped over one another's words trying to express their gratitude. Barbara held up a hand. The women quieted down.

"Now, if you'll excuse us," she said, "Slocum and I have some unfinished business." She reached for the first button on her shirt and popped it. Without a glance at the others, she kept going from button to button. By the time her shirt came off, they were gone, and the door was closed.

Stripping off her dungarees, she grinned, then leaned over him. Dangling her breasts in front of his astonished mouth, she teased him, rubbing the erect nipples against his lips.

Slocum pulled away and stood. He nearly fell over in his haste to shuck his own clothes. Barbara lay on the bed, her legs spread wide and one hand resting on her bush. Slocum watched her fingers part the already glistening lips. He knelt between her thighs and leaned forward. Her hand darted toward him, cool fingers closing on the rigid shaft.

He found the lips with the head of his cock, then slowly slid all the way in.

"Paradise isn't such a bad name for a hotel, after all," he said.

"Shut up and ride, cowboy," she whispered.